'Does Greg kiss you like that?

'Maybe you can't be completely confident of your real feelings without some form of comparison?'

The eye contact was locked on. Sophie couldn't have escaped even if she'd wanted to. And she didn't want to. But this was dangerous territory. The closest Sophie had come to real danger that she could think of. She cleared her throat nervously.

Oliver smiled. A lazy, slow smile that was almost predatory...as his lips brushed hers lightly.

Alison Roberts was born in New Zealand, and says she 'lived in London and Washington DC as a child, and began my working career as a primary school teacher. A lifelong interest in medicine was fostered by my doctor and nurse parents, flatting with doctors and physiotherapists on leaving home, and marriage to a house surgeon who is now a consultant cardiologist. I have also worked as a cardiology technician and research assistant. My husband's medical career took us to Glasgow for two years, which was an ideal place and time to start my writing career. I now live in Christchurch, New Zealand, with my husband, daughter and various pets.'

Recent titles by the same author:

DEFINITELY DADDY
A CHANGE OF HEART
PERFECT TIMING
MORE THAN A MISTRESS

AN IRRESISTIBLE INVITATION

BY
ALISON ROBERTS

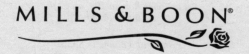

MILLS & BOON®

First published in Great Britain 2000
Harlequin Mills & Boon Limited,
Eton House, 18-24 Paradise Road, Richmond, Surrey TW9 1SR

© Alison Roberts 2000

ISBN 0 263 82260 5

Set in Times Roman 10½ on 12 pt.
03-0009-46333

Printed and bound in Spain
by Litografía Rosés, S.A., Barcelona

CHAPTER ONE

WAS now the right time to tell him?

The small car had become a trap. Sophie Bennett hadn't expected to see Oliver standing in the car park behind the old Christchurch house which had been converted into St David's Medical Centre. He smiled and waved, as though the sight of Sophie was exactly what Oliver Spencer had been expecting. As though he was waiting for her. She had to make her decision fast. Even at the snail's pace at which Sophie was moving, the manoeuvre to park couldn't last much longer.

Sophie pulled on the handbrake and reached for the ignition key to cut the engine. She sighed in exasperation as she noticed her fingers shaking slightly. This was quite ridiculous. It was no big deal, so why did she feel so nervous? Surreptitiously, Sophie tugged at the ring on her left hand.

'Ouch!' Sophie glared at her finger. How was she supposed to have noticed that all her indecisive twisting of the ring last night had made her finger swell? Not enough to be noticeable or cause any problems. Just enough to make it impossible to get the damned ring off with any ease. The ring she should no longer be wearing.

Oliver was walking towards her. He held a briefcase in one hand, and his jacket was slung casually over his arm. With his shirtsleeves already rolled up, Dr Spencer looked as calm and relaxed as he always

5

did. His thick, wavy hair had a permanently ruffled look, possibly caused by his casual habit of running his fingers through the dark waves. Along with his tanned skin and wide smile, the tousled look added to his untroubled-by-life demeanour. Oliver Spencer had probably never felt *really* nervous in his whole life, but Sophie's nerves were being stretched tighter with every step he took. She wished his smile wasn't quite so cheerful. She wished even harder that he wasn't opening her car door for her. She wasn't ready to get out. Not yet.

'Welcome back, Sophie!'

'I've only been away for the weekend,' Sophie said nervously. 'I never come in at the weekends.'

'Ah, but this weekend was different,' Oliver said meaningfully.

'I guess so.' Sophie turned to collect her bag.

'You *guess* so? How long is it since you and Garth had a weekend together?'

'Greg,' Sophie corrected automatically. Why couldn't Oliver ever remember her fiancé's name? Her *ex*-fiancé's name. 'Three months,' she added tonelessly. 'Ever since I started at St David's.'

'You don't sound very happy.' Oliver leaned closer. 'Wasn't *Greg* delighted to see you?'

'Of course he was.' Sophie swung her legs out of the car and Oliver stepped back a pace. Intelligent, dark grey eyes were observing her keenly. Oliver's eyes stood out as being his least laid-back feature. They missed nothing and they were interested in everything.

'And I was delighted to see him, too,' Sophie said as she stood up decisively. It was quite true, after all. She and Greg had a long history. They were good friends. But good friends were all they were ever going to be.

Oliver chuckled. 'I should hope so. Not much point getting married if you're not delighted to see each other.'

Tell him *now*, Sophie ordered herself. Before this goes any further. All it needs is a casual statement to the effect that she and Greg were no longer engaged. But what would she say when Oliver asked why she was still wearing her ring? Why *was* she still wearing her ring?

Oliver was watching her thoughtfully. 'I know I've said this many times, Sophie, but Garth *is* a very lucky man.' He shook his head sadly. 'I suppose I'll just have to distract myself by getting stuck into some work.' He extended his arm invitingly. 'After you, Dr Bennett.'

Sophie's tolerant smile was automatic. Her usual tactic of ignoring Oliver's flirting had become ingrained. It was just light-hearted fun, after all. Oliver Spencer never flirted with anyone else. Sophie Bennett—the happily engaged woman—was a safe target so it meant nothing. He'd probably run a mile if Sophie suddenly announced her changed status. Was that a more terrifying thought than the prospect of an opposite reaction? Which one was making her more nervous? Which one had persuaded her not to remove her ring quite yet so that she could buy a little time to ponder the repercussions?

Sophie skirted the old-fashioned woman's bicycle propped by the medical centre's front door. A large basket was attached to the handlebars and contained a loaf of what looked like exceptionally healthy bread. No. Now was not the right time to tell Oliver.

They had patients waiting and Sophie Bennett was more than happy to postpone her own agenda.

'Morning, Sophie. Morning, Oliver.' Toni Marsh, St David's practice manager, paused, before answering the telephone. 'How was Auckland, Sophie?'

'Wet,' Sophie responded promptly. 'It rained non-stop.'

'Didn't dampen the enthusiasm, though,' Oliver reported.

'I should hope not,' Toni said briskly. She turned her attention to the phone call.

Sophie surveyed Toni's domain as she crossed the reception area. The toys were still neatly piled in the big wicker basket, the magazines tidily stacked on the various coffee-tables. Morning surgery hours weren't due to start for another fifteen minutes but an elderly couple sat near the reception desk and looked up hopefully as the two doctors crossed the room. Another woman was sitting in the corner of the waiting room, cross-legged, in a large armchair. Her eyes were shut and her hands lay on her legs, palms upward, fingers and thumbs forming enclosed circles. Like rings. Sophie sighed audibly. Oliver frowned with concern, followed the line of her gaze and then winked at Sophie.

'Know any good mantras?' he whispered.

'I wish I did,' Sophie murmured. 'I could use one right now.'

'I thought you seemed a bit tense.' Oliver stared at Sophie intently and then leaned over the large semi-circular counter that separated the waiting area from the main office. 'Don't you think Sophie looks a bit tense, Toni?'

Toni glanced anxiously at Sophie who grinned and

rolled her eyes to indicate that Oliver's concern was unfounded. Toni smiled wickedly as she adjusted the telephone receiver she was still holding and reached for a pencil. 'Would ten-fifteen suit you, Mr Collins? Dr Spencer has an appointment free then.'

Oliver shook his head frantically, holding up his hands in a signal to stop. Toni smiled sweetly, reaching to answer the second telephone as she continued talking. 'Yes, do bring the sample in, Mr Collins. A jam jar is just fine. Dr Spencer will appreciate your forethought. Yes—ten-fifteen.' Toni smoothly transferred her ear to the other telephone. 'Good morning. St David's Medical Centre. Toni speaking.'

'Sophie?'

The calculating tone in Oliver Spencer's voice was reassuringly familiar. Much to Sophie's relief, his interest in her emotional well-being had been overridden by a more pressing concern. Sophie smiled with genuine amusement as she shook her head firmly and ducked into the first door past the treatment room.

'Mr Collins is a wonderful patient for a GP registrar.' Oliver had followed Sophie into her consulting room. 'He has everything you can think of wrong with him. He's spent seventy years studying the *Reader's Digest Guide to Good Health*.' Oliver smiled cunningly. 'God knows what he's got in the jam jar today but I'm sure it's absolutely fascinating.'

'I'm sure it is.' Sophie was beginning to feel much better. She dropped her shoulder-bag beside her desk and lifted her white coat from the back of her chair. 'You can tell me all about it at morning teatime.'

'No.' Oliver looked vaguely alarmed. 'Mr Collins's samples are best avoided at any time when you're planning to eat.' He glanced back into the corridor.

'Josh!' he announced happily. 'Just the person I wanted to see.'

'No, Oliver.' The firm tone couldn't disguise the amusement evident in Dr Cooper's face. 'I do not want to see Mr Collins and I especially do not want to see whatever's in that jam jar.' He turned to Sophie. 'How are you, Sophie?'

'Fine, thanks.' Sophie straightened her coat. 'I'd better go and see who Toni has lined up for me.' A baby's cry could now be heard in the waiting area. 'Sounds like we might be in for a busy day.'

'When isn't Monday busy?' Josh was still blocking her doorway. 'How was Auckland?' he asked with interest. 'I'll bet Greg was rather pleased to see you.'

'Sophie doesn't want to talk about it,' Oliver informed his senior partner. 'She's a bit tense.'

'I am not!' Sophie was exasperated. 'I don't know why everybody is so interested in my weekend. It was no big deal.'

'It was to me,' Oliver confided to Josh. 'There I was, hoping Sophie would come back minus her engagement ring.'

Josh Cooper laughed. 'What, having decided that Greg doesn't measure up now that she's had a dose of your charm?'

'Exactly!' Oliver sighed dramatically. 'But there it is—still firmly on her finger. I can't understand it.'

'I can.' Josh winked at Sophie who found herself blushing. What would her colleagues say if they knew how close to the truth they actually were? She couldn't understand why the ring was still on her finger either. What was so terrifying about admitting the changes the weekend had produced? The decision had been hers after all. It wasn't as if it was some kind of personal failing. And surely nobody would assume she was interested in Oliver. Would they? Or more particularly—would Oliver?

Josh was looking thoughtfully at Oliver. 'You know, it *is* about time you got some romance in your life.'

'I know,' Oliver nodded sadly. 'That's all my mother could talk about when I took her out to lunch yesterday. I have a duty as an only child to produce grandchildren before she's too decrepit to enjoy them.'

'How old is your mother, Oliver?' Sophie queried suspiciously.

'Fifty-six. But she's going downhill fast. She only goes to aerobics five days a week now.' Oliver grinned at Sophie. 'Would you like to meet my mother? She'd love to meet you.'

Josh shook his head admonishingly. 'You should try your charms on someone who's in a position to reciprocate and then you might actually get off first base.'

'Who did you have in mind, Josh?' It was Oliver's turn to look suspicious. 'I don't want one of your cast-offs, however rich the choice might be.'

Josh grinned. 'My women are too sophisticated for the likes of you, Dr Spencer. Did you see that gypsy in the corner of the waiting room—with all the bangles and that gorgeous wild hair? She looks more your type.'

Sophie reached into her coat pocket at the reminder and quickly scooped back her shoulder-length straight hair, winding the scrunchy to hold her dark blonde tresses in a neat ponytail. She wondered how Oliver would react to the suggestion. Not that he would consider dating a patient, but did Josh know something that she didn't regarding his taste in women?

'Hmm.' Oliver's tone was calculating again. 'You could be right. Swap you for Mr Collins.'

Josh laughed again. 'No way. Not that I have any say in the matter, anyway. She wants Sophie. Toni said she was standing outside with her bicycle when she got to work this morning and she was prepared to wait as long as it took but Dr Bennett was whom she intended to see.'

'I'd better not keep her waiting any longer, then,' Sophie said briskly. She walked away from the two men with relief. She didn't want to hear any more about the type of women that might interest Dr Spencer. Neither did she want any more interest shown in her weekend. Not by Josh and not by Oliver. Especially not by Oliver.

Oliver Spencer watched his registrar head purposefully away. So, the gypsy wanted Sophie, did she? He could understand that. Sophie Bennett was an extremely desirable woman. Intelligence shone from those dark blue eyes and silky, soft-looking straight hair framed a face that was surprisingly innocent for someone her age. A face that advertised compassion and honesty. Sophie also had a quite delicious-looking mouth that smiled frequently and easily and small, delicate hands that were as competent as her brain. Sophie Bennett looked like the girl next door. She even had a faint dusting of freckles on her small, slightly snub nose. She was exactly the type of woman his mother had always hoped he would find, but Sophie Bennett had already found someone else. Long ago.

Oliver really *had* hoped that this weekend might

have changed something. Had he been wrong in thinking that the attraction that had escalated over the last three months had not been entirely one-sided? He'd kept things light. He wasn't going to break up a happy couple. No way! But many a true word was spoken in jest and if he'd had any real indication that his admiration was unwelcome he would have stopped.

Sophie *did* seem tense. Had she had a row with Greg? Oliver sighed, trying to suppress the ignoble hope that there had been some major friction. He'd never been troubled by jealousy before but this weekend had been an unpleasant introduction to the emotion. The gypsy wanted Sophie. Greg wanted Sophie.

So did Oliver Spencer.

As Sophie entered the main office, separated from the waiting area by the large semi-circular counter, she bumped shoulders with the hurrying figure of St David's other full-time staff member.

'Sorry, Sophie.' Janet Muir's face was creased worriedly.

'What's up, Janet?'

The practice nurse sighed with frustration. 'The new batch of flu vaccine was supposed to be here first thing this morning.' The Scottish burr in Janet's voice was always more pronounced when she was agitated. 'We're going to be inundated after that scare on the news last night about the Hong Kong outbreak and we're nearly out of supplies.'

Toni Marsh was holding a phone receiver against her shoulder. 'I've got the couriers on the line,' she soothed Janet. 'I'm just sorting it out.' Toni waved towards the end of the counter. 'New patient for you, Sophie. I've made up a file.'

Sophie picked up the flat, clean folder. The name and coded number were already printed on its cover, the consultation notes sheet clipped inside with a computer printout giving patient details. No reason for the consultation had been given. Sophie stepped into the open archway that divided the waiting room from the main corridor.

'Miss Ellis?'

The gypsy's eyes opened smartly. She rose from her cross-legged position with graceful ease and her long, layered skirt rippled as she moved, prompting Sophie to wonder how on earth she managed to ride a bicycle in such attire.

'Call me Pagan,' the woman invited warmly.

Sophie smiled. Pagan Ellis looked the picture of health. She also looked very friendly and far more interesting than many of Sophie's patients. Perhaps today wouldn't be so bad after all.

'Would you like to come this way, Pagan?'

Pagan's impressive collection of jewellery jangled musically as she settled herself into the chair. 'Is it OK if I call you Sophie? I'm not big on formal stuff.'

'Sure.' Sophie closed the door and then sat at her desk, opening the new file in front of her. 'This is your first visit to St David's, isn't it?'

'Oh, yes.' Pagan Ellis was gazing around Sophie's consulting room. She nodded to herself.

'What can I help you with, Pagan?'

'Are you a Virgo, Sophie?'

'Sorry?'

'Your sun sign. You know, your zodiac sign?'

Pagan's full mouth twitched impatiently. 'When's your birthday?'

'September tenth.' Sophie's astonishment made her respond without question.

'I knew it!' Pagan said triumphantly. 'You're pure Virgo.'

'Really?' Sophie was intrigued. This might not be a textbook example of how to initiate a consultation but the invitation was too tempting to resist.

'Everything's so tidy.' Pagan nodded. 'You make order out of chaos. I'll bet you write lists of things to do every day.'

Sophie couldn't help smiling. She had quite a long list tucked into her shoulder-bag.

'You enjoy books.' Pagan's bangles clinked as she waved at Sophie's shelf of medical textbooks. 'You do work that is challenging and I'll bet you're a per-fectionist.'

'I like to be thorough,' Sophie admitted.

'And organised,' Pagan added. 'You've probably got your future all planned out and shaping up exactly how you want it.'

Sophie's intrigue with the potential clairvoyance of her patient evaporated. She might be right about having her future planned out but as for shaping up... Sophie didn't need the reminder of the plug she had just pulled out in that direction.

'I wouldn't say that exactly.' Sophie's tone was cooler. More professional. 'Now, about you, Pagan. What brings you—?'

'Oh, I'm an Aquarius,' Pagan interrupted. 'Pretty obvious, eh?'

'Ah...'

'Did you know we're actually in the age of Aquarius?'

'No,' Sophie said slowly. She took a furtive glance at her watch and succeeded only in catching sight of her engagement ring.

'Uranus dropped into the sign in 1995,' Pagan confirmed happily. 'It won't leave until 2004. Did you know that the Internet started in 1995 and that WWW is also the logo for Aquarius?'

'No,' Sophie said more firmly. 'And I don't think—'

'That was how I found him,' Pagan said brightly. 'On the Internet. Couldn't be more appropriate really, could it?'

'I really couldn't—'

'I mean, our signs were perfectly matched. I knew he was going to be the father of my baby.' Pagan smiled blissfully. 'It was wonderful. We met up in Hawaii and made love on the beach to the sound of the waves. Conceived in Pisces—that's a water sign, of course. And it's due in Scorpio. Another water sign.' Pagan sighed rapturously.

'Ah...so you're pregnant?' Sophie reached for a pen. 'Is that why you've come to see me?'

'Of course.'

Sophie nodded. Finally, they were getting somewhere. 'What was the date of the first day of your last period?'

'That would have been the sixth of February. Conception was February the twentieth. Really the cusp of Pisces and Aquarius. That's my sign, you know.'

'So you said.' Sophie nodded a little wearily.

'You're about eleven weeks pregnant, then. Have you been to a doctor since you missed your first period?'

'No. I had to find just the right person.' Pagan smiled warmly at Sophie. 'I've been to see a few but nobody had the right aura.' She gazed at Sophie intently. 'You do. I want you to deliver my child.'

'We don't do deliveries, exactly,' Sophie said apologetically. 'It's more shared care with a midwife and an obstetrician. We do a lot of the routine antenatal checks and—'

'I've got a midwife,' Pagan interrupted. 'She's great. It was her idea that we find the right doctor. Just in case.'

Sophie's gaze had slipped to the computer printout. 'You're thirty-seven, is that right?'

Pagan nodded.

'And this is your first baby?'

'My only baby.'

'We'll need to book you in for a scan. Have you considered amniocentesis at all?'

'What's that?' Pagan's eyes narrowed suspiciously.

'It's a test that can detect a range of birth defects, including spina bifida and Down's syndrome.' Sophie pulled a book down from her shelf and flicked the pages rapidly. 'Down's syndrome is the result of a chromosomal abnormality in the baby. Maternal age is an important factor and if you look at this graph here you can see that the risk rises sharply after the age of thirty-five.' Sophie turned the book to face her patient. 'The test involves removing a small amount of the amniotic fluid that surrounds the baby in the womb. It's usually done at around fourteen to sixteen weeks when there is more fluid available.'

Pagan Ellis gave the textbook no more than a dismissive glance. 'Don't fancy that. I don't want any interventions. This pregnancy is going to be totally natural.' She shrugged. 'Theoretically, I suppose I should have gone for a test tube baby. I mean the age of Aquarius is all about technology but some things are meant to be natural.' Pagan grinned. 'More fun that way.'

Sophie was not going to be sidetracked. 'Do you have any family history of genetic problems?'

'No.'

'What about the father's family history?'

'God, Ziggy and I never talked about things like that.' Pagan gave Sophie a disappointed stare. 'It's not as if he's going to have anything to do with the baby.' She grinned again. 'Mind you, he said it had been a blast and if I ever wanted another kid to give him a bell. No,' Pagan finished decisively. 'No tests. I want a natural pregnancy and a natural birth. A very special birth.'

Sophie cleared her throat, hoping that the prickle of alarm she felt was unfounded. 'Just what did you have in mind for the birth, Pagan?'

'A beach, of course,' Pagan replied kindly. 'I thought you understood. Water signs and all that, you know?'

'A beach?'

'Well, not *exactly*.' Pagan leaned forward. 'I really mean the sea.'

'Apparently, the surf will speed up contractions. Her faith healer is all in favour of it.' Sophie finally sipped at her mug of coffee as she finished her tale of woe. 'What on earth am I going to do, Oliver?'

Oliver Spencer was smiling broadly. Sophie could

see the delight in the way the lines around his eyes
crinkled, the rather lopsided tilt to his mouth and the
way his head tipped back a little as he ran long fingers
through the waves of dark hair. She blinked, disconcerted at her easy recognition of Oliver's response.
She had only known the man for three months but
she could predict exactly the supportive comment he
was about to make.

'It's early days,' Oliver said cheerfully. 'You'll talk
her out of it.'

'I think I should hand her over to you. You're my
supervisor after all. GP registrars are supposed to
hand over the really tricky cases.'

'Not at all.' Oliver sat back, looking totally relaxed.
His shirtsleeves were still rolled up and his tie knotted
only loosely around his neck. They were both sitting
in the staffroom at the back of the house. Originally
the kitchen and dining room of a family home, the
dividing wall had been knocked out, making a spa-
cious area with comfortable couches and a dining
table. The kitchen facilities had been kept, along with
an extra refrigerator to house drugs and specimens
that needed to be kept cool. Sophie wondered if Mr
Collins's jam jar was hiding in the fridge.

'It's my responsibility to provide guidance. To
make sure you have the facilities and support you
need and to be available to bail you out when you
have real problems. Have I ever let you down?'

'No.' Sophie's smile reflected very genuine grati-
tude. Oliver Spencer had been wonderful. Too wonderful. He had been welcoming, totally supportive
and generous with his time and cheerful enthusiasm
as he oversaw her training. His appreciation of Sophie
might have been disconcerting at first but she had

become used to it surprisingly quickly. At what point had she started wanting to respond? Sophie squashed the dangerous line of thought.

'Besides...' Oliver's mouth twitched '...Pagan Ellis is quite right.'

'What?' Sophie's eyes widened dramatically.

'You've got the right aura.' Oliver was smiling but there was a glint in his eyes that gave Sophie a now familiar internal twinge. 'I knew it all along, of course, but it's nice to have it confirmed by an expert.'

Janet Muir bustled into the staffroom, carrying a small carton. 'They've finally arrived,' she announced. 'And not a minute too soon. I've got at least twenty people coming in for flu shots this afternoon.' She threw open the door of the storage fridge. 'Och,' she exclaimed in disgust. 'What is *that*?'

'Is it in a jam jar?' Oliver queried calmly.

'Aye.' Janet was staring intently into the interior of the fridge.

'Don't ask, then,' Oliver advised. 'Unless you really want to find out.'

'I don't think I do.' Janet began unloading her carton. 'It's put me right off my lunch already.' She glanced up. 'Have you had lunch, Sophie?'

'I'm just having coffee. I got way behind, thanks to my first consultation, and I'm still trying to catch up.'

'How was your weekend?'

'Great, thanks.' Sophie could feel the ring constricting her finger again. 'How was yours?'

'Awful.' Janet shut the fridge door and sighed. 'The boys broke the front window and then it started pouring and I had to get a glazier to come and fix it on Sunday. It cost twice as much and the carpet's still soaked. I put the heater on but there's a funny smell.'

'How did the window get broken?'

Janet reached for a mug and a teabag. 'Apparently, by an act of divine intervention. Never mind the fact that there was a cricket bat on the lawn and a cricket ball on the carpet. The boys swore it wasn't them.'

'You mean they lied about it?' Oliver was frowning.

'It's becoming the first line of defence.' Janet sighed again. 'They back each other up and they're amazingly convincing.'

Sophie smiled. She could just imagine Janet's six-year-old twin boys, with their curly blonde hair framing angelic faces, denying yet another misdeed. They were apparently a real handful but Janet seemed to cope admirably with single motherhood.

Oliver was still frowning. 'What did you do about it?'

'Well, the window's fixed now and I suppose it wasn't really their fault. The garden's too small to play cricket in and I was too busy to take them to the park.' Janet added two spoons of sugar to her mug.

'I meant about the lying.' Oliver stood up. 'That's a lot worse than breaking the window.'

'I know.' Janet looked anxious. 'I don't know what to do. It's so obvious it's funny. We all ended up laughing about it.'

'Lying's never funny,' Oliver stated. 'It might be obvious at the moment but they'll get better at it. You need to do something about it now, Janet.' For some inexplicable reason Oliver's gaze locked onto Sophie's. 'Take my word for it,' he said seriously. 'Honesty is far too important to compromise.'

Sophie shifted uncomfortably and her eyes slid away from Oliver's as she tucked her left hand inside her pocket. It was all very well for Oliver to preach. He didn't have complications like boisterous twin sons to raise alone. Or the image of being a happily engaged woman suddenly shattered.

Toni Marsh came into the room, carrying a packet of sandwiches and an apple. 'I still haven't got the waiting room empty,' she groaned. 'I'm just taking five minutes. Why are Mondays so busy?'

'Nobody wants to use the after-hours practice on weekends,' Oliver observed. 'They like us too much.'

Toni pushed the wire frames of her spectacles more firmly into place on her nose. 'Perhaps you could start being rude to a few people, then.'

'I'll see what I can do,' Oliver promised. 'But you'll have to work on Sophie. Her aura's too good.'

'Her what?'

'Never mind.' Sophie rose to her feet to follow Oliver. 'It's about as believable as Oliver being rude to patients. Is there anyone out there for me?'

Toni nodded, hastily swallowing her mouthful of sandwich. 'Lily Weymouth has brought her baby in. He's running a temperature and is pretty miserable. I put her in the side room so she could try and feed him.'

Sophie nodded. 'Probably another ear infection. He had one last month.'

'And there's Mrs Bell. I think she's got the flu.'

Janet's yoghurt spoon paused halfway to her mouth. 'You've had your flu shot, haven't you, Sophie?'

'Yes, last week. You gave it to me, remember?'

'Oh, aye.' Janet nodded and then smiled. 'Seems like a long time ago somehow.'

It did seem a long time ago. There had been a lot of water under the bridge since then. The current seemed to have increased its speed. More worryingly, it had completely changed direction. No wonder Sophie felt suddenly adrift.

In retrospect, the change had been coming for a long time. It wasn't really her fault. It wasn't Greg's fault either. Sophie knew exactly where to lay the blame for the catalyst of her life's disruption.

It was all Oliver Spencer's fault.

CHAPTER TWO

OF COURSE, it was Oliver Spencer's fault.

Why hadn't it occurred to Sophie earlier? In between sessions in a long afternoon of peering down undersized ear canals, swabbing sore throats and dispensing some much-needed dietary advice, the issue clarified itself with satisfying logic.

It was Oliver Spencer's fault because he was too nice. Too young, too attractive and far too easygoing. If she had taken up a position as a GP registrar with a supervisor who was middle-aged, overweight, bald and grumpy then she wouldn't be in this predicament.

Then again, she didn't blame Josh Cooper and he was perfectly nice as well. At thirty-four, Oliver was four years younger than Josh. Both the doctors were tall, dark and good-looking. They were both intelligent and had a good sense of humour. They were both highly skilled doctors. It was no wonder that patient numbers at St David's were steadily increasing. There was more than enough work for a keen GP trainee. Oliver and Josh were starting to talk about the need for a third full-time partner.

Oliver had been married once but his divorce was apparently ancient history. Josh swore he'd never even been remotely tempted by the state of matrimony. They were both perfectly eligible bachelors and they had both been quite open about their appreciation of the addition Sophie Bennett had made to the staff of St David's. The three doctors all got along

very well which had been an added bonus, though
Oliver was definitely more laid back. Sophie suspected it might be because he didn't have to cope with
as many late nights and hangovers as Josh seemed to,
but what did she really know about his social life?
Perhaps Oliver's tolerance levels were better than his
senior partner's.

Had she just spent too much time alone with Oliver
while finding her feet in a new environment? No.
Even Josh had noticed there was something between
her and his junior partner that excluded him. He had
gone as far as to warn Oliver off.

'Don't stay too late,' he'd teasingly admonished as
he'd headed home, leaving them alone for yet another
tutorial session during those early weeks. 'Just remember that Sophie's a happily engaged woman.'

Had she been? Even then? Would a happily engaged woman have felt that very physical buzz at
knowing someone found her attractive? Maybe. And
maybe Oliver's freely given approval as Sophie made
the start on the career she had always wanted was
something she had been starved of. Her father certainly wasn't giving her any and Greg had been angry
at her decision to take up this position so far away,
however much he had tried to hide it.

A happily engaged woman would not, however,
have found the attraction exciting. Would not have
felt even the slightest desire to encourage it. Sophie
had been thoroughly ashamed of exactly that desire.
The protection of her ring had been welcome. A
talisman against change. Against feelings that were
new enough to be frightening, their potential power
an unknown and very unsettling force. *That* was why

she had hesitated in removing the ring. Why it was so difficult. She still needed protection.

Yes. It was Oliver's fault for being so attractive. For stirring depths in Sophie that Greg had never more than touched the surface of. For making Sophie wonder whether those depths might, in fact, be better off for a bit of stirring.

Sophie's last patient for the day was Ruby Murdock. Ruby had been one of Sophie's first patients when she'd arrived at St David's and this was the third visit. Ruby was what Sophie considered to be an excellent example of a general practice patient. Aged sixty-seven, widowed but with devoted family support from her daughter, Ruby had a variety of medical problems.

A broken ankle some four years previously had curtailed her level of physical activity significantly and her weight had increased steadily. Two years ago Ruby had broken her wrist which had reduced her activity even further. She had also developed late onset asthma. Her blood pressure had crept up and was now borderline for therapy and Ruby experienced the odd twinge of chest pain which was probably not angina but needed monitoring. Her weight was still increasing but Ruby remained cheerfully optimistic that she could get on top of the problem.

In fact, Ruby was always cheerful. Sophie also considered her patient to be an excellent example of the motherly type—rather short, now decidedly plump, grey-haired and amiable. It was easy to imagine that she might have ruled over a large brood of offspring and was now surrounded by an increasing number of adoring grandchildren. But Ruby had had only one daughter on whom to lavish her maternal abilities and the total of grandchildren was only three.

Sophie was pleased that Ruby was her final patient for Monday afternoon. She could relax without the pressures of time restraints and enjoy Ruby's companionable chatter. Ruby Murdock loved to talk. She was still answering Sophie's query about how the family was as she settled herself more comfortably in her chair beside Sophie's desk.

'So Nathan and Tim have both started playing soccer. I'm so pleased they don't want to play rugby. Such a dangerous sport and they're all such *rough* people!' Ruby's handbag was positioned carefully beside her feet with an extra nudge to straighten it. 'Of course, it is a little awkward. Felicity has to take them to practice on Wednesday afternoons after school and that means we have to hurry through our shopping. Wednesday afternoon is when she takes me to the supermarket.'

'Your daughter is a big help to you, isn't she, Mrs Murdock?'

'Oh, yes, dear.' Ruby Murdock's face relaxed into a contented smile. 'She's a good girl. I really couldn't manage without her. Especially not now.'

'How's the asthma been since I last saw you?' Sophie queried. 'Did you bring your peak-flow diary in to show me?'

The handbag was retrieved but Ruby looked embarrassed as she rummaged in its depths. 'I'm afraid I haven't kept it up terribly well. It's so hard to remember every morning.'

'Are you remembering to use your Flixotide inhaler twice a day?'

'When I need to—of course I do. And I'm sure I'm

inhaling correctly. That spacer thing is much easier and your lesson last time was very helpful.'

Sophie's smile was a little distracted. 'That's good, Mrs Murdock, but the Flixotide is the inhaler you use to prevent problems, not treat them. Remember how I explained about the airways being inflamed and that makes them more likely to react and cause an asthma attack? We need to treat the inflammation *all* the time. That way you shouldn't need to use your broncho-dilator—that's the Ventolin inhaler—nearly as often.'

Ruby was nodding and smiling. 'Maybe I'll bring Felicity in with me next time. If I tell her what I need to remember then she makes sure I do. She just dropped me off today because she had to collect Brent from the airport. She's given me some money to get a taxi home.'

Sophie was looking at the peak-flow diary. Over a period of three weeks only half a dozen of the spaces had been filled. 'Are you still being woken from sleep with coughing or wheezing?'

'Oh, yes. I haven't had a good night's sleep in weeks. I'm that tired.' Ruby wagged her head with concern. 'You look rather tired yourself today, dear.'

'It's been a long day,' Sophie admitted. 'But I'm fine, thanks.'

'You young things seem to be able to cope with anything. My Felicity is so busy all the time. She never stops. She'll be thirty-four soon but you wouldn't think so, the way she dashes about. How old are you, dear?'

'Twenty-six.'

'Oh, my! And you have such a responsible job. Such long hours.'

'I always wanted to be a doctor,' Sophie said

firmly. 'It's exactly the right career for me. I love the responsibility and I don't mind the hours. Tell me, does your wheeziness or shortness of breath mean you've been any more limited in what you can do since I last saw you?'

Ruby nodded sadly. 'I don't seem to be able to do very much at all at the moment. I even got Felicity to go the library for me this week and I've *always* done that by myself.'

'How many times have you used your Ventolin inhaler this week?'

'Oh, every day, dear. Sometimes more than once.'

Sophie was scribbling a note. Perhaps she'd better have a word with Felicity. Ruby's preventative therapy needed to be firmly established and her control assessed far more accurately. She reached for her stethoscope. 'Could you unbutton your cardigan for me, please, Mrs Murdock? I want to have a listen to your chest.'

The task was completed slowly. Ruby's wrist was still stiff as a result of her fracture two years previously. Sophie suspected that the physiotherapy advice hadn't been consistently followed. She fiddled with her stethoscope as she waited patiently.

'That's a lovely ring, dear. How long have you been engaged?'

'Quite a while.' Sophie's response was brisk. This was not a line of conversation she wanted to pursue.

'And when are you getting married?'

'I'm not sure. Would you like some help with those buttons?'

'Oh, no. I can manage,' Ruby stated valiantly. She finished with the cardigan and began on her dress buttons. 'What does your fiancé do, then, dear? Is he another doctor?'

'Mmm.' It was the only response Sophie could manage through her gritted teeth.

'Isn't that perfect?' Mrs Murdock beamed. 'You'll be able to work together. You can always do it part time when the children are young. Just perfect!'

Sophie jammed the stethoscope earpieces into place. 'Don't talk now, Mrs Murdock. Try and take some nice deep breaths for me.'

It was time Sophie went home. Ruby Murdock's taxi had arrived promptly and Sophie's worry that she had been too stern at the end of the consultation had been mitigated by her patient's cheerful leave-taking and promises to comply with all the advice she had received.

The waiting room was now empty. Janet had rushed off on the dot of 5 p.m. to collect the boys from the babysitter who took them after school. Toni looked exhausted. She was rubbing at her eyes, her spectacles pushed up on her forehead, as she hovered over the fax machine which was spitting out what looked like lab results. Oliver and Josh were both in the office as well. Josh was looking over Toni's shoulder at the emerging results. Oliver was sitting at Toni's desk, scribbling notes in a patient file.

'You really should go back to the optometrist,' Josh was telling Toni. 'You probably need new glasses. Why don't you have a go with contact lenses?'

'My eyes won't tolerate them,' Toni said dismally. 'I've got an appointment this evening to see if I need an upgrade. I should say a downgrade. At this rate my lenses will get so thick nobody will even remember I've got eyes at all.'

'Oh, come on.' Josh gave Toni's shoulder a friendly squeeze. 'You look great with specs. Intelligent and very—'

Josh's compliment was cut off as the outside door opened and everyone glanced up in dismay. An emergency at 5.30 p.m. on a Monday would be just too much. The red and white shirt of the newcomer advertised his mission.

'Back again, Ross?' Toni shook her head. 'You can't keep away from us. You've already taken all today's samples.'

'This is different.' The courier smiled triumphantly as he produced the sheaf of red roses from behind his back.

'Oh, for me? Ross, you shouldn't have.' Toni's grin revealed her lack of sincerity.

Josh smiled sympathetically. 'Sorry, Swampy, but it must be some birthday blooms for yours truly.' He sighed in satisfaction. 'I guess somebody loves me after all. I wonder who?'

'Take your pick,' Toni muttered. The use of the nickname had clearly irritated her. 'There are plenty to choose from.'

The courier was shaking his head. 'Sorry, guys, but these are for one Dr Sophie Bennett. Special delivery and almost too late. Could you sign here for me, please, Dr Bennett?'

'Sure.' Sophie stepped forward eagerly. The roses had to be from Greg. Perhaps she *had* been wrong in gently rebuffing Greg's claim that their long-standing friendship was more than enough of a base to build a marriage on. That long-term commitment needed exactly such a base. That the kind of passionate relationship she was talking about didn't really exist, or if it did it couldn't last. Right now Sophie was almost willing to concede her decision had been an error. To duck back into safe territory and leave her ring exactly where it was. She pulled the card from its tiny envelope.

'Some decisions are too difficult to make without a push. You were right. Miss you. Love you. Greg'

Sophie buried her nose in the velvety dark blooms to hide her disappointment. And the fear that a safe refuge had just been denied her. Toni stroked one of the petals.

'These are gorgeous,' she breathed. 'And *so* romantic.'

'I knew it had been a memorable weekend.' Oliver's tone was almost disappointed.

'Oh, it was,' Sophie murmured. She kept her face screened by the bouquet as she fought back the prickle of threatened tears.

'How long did you say you'd been engaged?' The query came from Oliver and his tone suggested that Sophie was being watched closely.

'Five years,' she muttered. 'Since second year in med school.'

'And you met at high school,' Toni said with awe. 'Genuine childhood sweethearts. It's hard to believe it can actually happen.'

'Sure is.' Josh didn't sound the least bit impressed. 'Do you mean to say you've never even been *out* with another man, Sophie?'

'No. Only Greg.' Sophie wondered how long one could look fascinated by a bunch of flowers without raising suspicion. She glanced at Josh and smiled brightly. 'I was never interested in anyone else.'

'That's *so* romantic,' Toni sighed.

'That's *so* stupid,' Josh contradicted.

'Why?' Toni and Sophie both spoke together.

'Well, how can you possibly know he's the right person for you? How can you make a sound decision without even trying to make some sort of a comparison?'

Sophie frowned. It was precisely part of the same doubts she had harboured for so long herself but somehow, coming from Josh, it made the argument seem shallow. An excuse for playing the field without consideration of the potential effects. Toni appeared to agree. The sound she made was dismissive.

'Has it ever occurred to you, Dr Cooper, that it's possible to confuse the issue with *too* much data?'

Sophie grinned. The legion of Josh Cooper's ex-girlfriends had become part of St David's folklore. Some of the phone calls she knew Toni was obliged to field were quite enough to justify the practice manager's acerbic comment. She felt inclined to support her.

'When you meet the right person you just know,' she asserted.

'Not when you're fifteen years old,' Josh snorted.

'I was seventeen,' Sophie defended herself.

'How do you know exactly?' Oliver asked with keen interest. 'When you meet the right person?'

Sophie made the mistake of meeting his gaze and to her horror she found herself blushing. Here she was defending her inexperience and loyalty to a relationship that didn't exist any more. She was virtually lying to the man who had warned her only hours ago that honesty was far too important to compromise. A man who just needed to look at her the way he was doing right now to induce a wave of physical response enough to make her toes curl.

'I… Ah…' Completely flustered, Sophie adjusted her grip on the bunch of roses. The card slipped from her fingers and sailed onto the floor. She crouched swiftly, but not fast enough to prevent Oliver picking up the card first. The time it took for him to hand it to her was more than enough for him to register the handwritten message.

They were both crouched on the floor, their knees only an inch or two apart. Sophie's breath caught. Oliver's gaze was questioning. Almost hopeful. Sophie's heart rate increased sharply. She only hoped she didn't look as vulnerable as she felt.

'A difficult decision?' Oliver enquired softly. His gaze dropped to her left hand and then returned to her face. 'What were you right about, Sophie?'

Oh, God. Maybe if they'd been alone, Sophie could have told the truth. Could have taken the plunge into the unknown territory that Oliver Spencer represented. Unknown. Potentially dangerous. Definitely exciting. But they weren't alone and Sophie felt trapped by the web she had successfully woven about herself and had reinforced only minutes ago. The myth of the happily engaged woman. The woman who had known she had met the right person even if she had only been seventeen years old. Her voice seemed to be coming from a long way away.

'The wedding date,' she heard herself saying. 'We… I finally made a decision.'

'Really?' Toni sounded excited. 'Oh, I love weddings! When is it going to be, Sophie?'

'July.' Sophie closed her eyes briefly. Why on earth had she said that? Her runaway mouth refused to close itself. 'July twenty-fifth,' she added for good measure.

Oliver was still crouched beside her. He frowned as though puzzled but then his expression changed to one of bland neutrality. 'Congratulations,' he murmured. 'If that's *really* what you want.'

'Of course it is.' Sophie straightened, clutching the roses tightly.

'That's only three months away,' Josh observed. 'You're not planning on leaving us before you sit your Primex exams and qualify as a registered GP, are you?'

'No.' Sophie bit her lip. 'Of course not.' She had forgotten that she would be in Christchurch at least until the end of October to finish her GP training programme. Why hadn't she picked a date next year? Why had she picked a damned date at all?

'So you're going to get married and then live in separate cities?' Oliver sounded intrigued rather than critical.

'No. Well, not for long anyway.' Sophie felt a desperate need to escape. 'I'd better get going. I want to ring Greg and thank him for the flowers and I've got a lot of reading I want to get done before the workshop on Wednesday afternoon. It's the one on minor surgery.' Sophie knew she was babbling. 'I've been really looking forward to this one.'

'See you tomorrow, then.' Josh had turned his attention back to the fax he was holding. 'Just look at that serum cholesterol level. Nine-point-eight! Phew!'

Oliver said nothing. He was staring at Sophie with an expression that hinted strongly of disapproval.

Toni leaned over the counter as Sophie reached the front door.

'We'll talk tomorrow,' she said happily. 'I want to hear all about your plans. Especially your wedding dress.'

The ring had to come off. It *had* to. The roses lay abandoned on the kitchen bench as Sophie squirted a generous dollop of dishwashing liquid onto her finger. She gripped the gold band and stared at the small solitaire diamond, a poignant stab reminding her of the pride with which the ring had first been worn. It had been a symbol of a future—dreamed about, carefully planned and striven for. A future that no longer existed. Perhaps it had only ever been a fantasy. Sophie pulled the ring and found it slipped off far more easily than she had expected. She placed it beside the bouquet of flowers and rinsed her soapy hands. Then she reached for a tumbler and filled it from the box of wine that sat in her fridge. She didn't normally have a drink after work but she was in dire need of something tonight. She was very glad that she had carried her glass with her when she moved to answer the telephone a minute later.

'Hi, Dad.' She took a large swallow of the chilled white wine. It tasted of cardboard. She should have bought a bottle to celebrate moving to Christchurch, not a five-litre cardboard carafe. Now it even had a faint aftertaste of dishwashing liquid. 'Sorry, Dad.' Sophie tried to forget the wine. 'I didn't hear that. How are you?'

'How I am is not why I'm ringing.' As usual, her father got straight to the point. 'I was talking to Greg this morning. He informs me you've broken off your engagement.'

Sophie took a deep breath. 'That's right, Dad. I have.'

'I thought you might come to your senses after Greg took up his registrar position and decided to specialise. Surely three months of infected ears, geriatrics, overweight women and social work with people who just want to be patients has been enough to show you what general practice is all about.'

'Yes, it has.' Sophie drained her glass. Cardboard and soap weren't too bad when you got used to them. 'I love it. It's what I want to do, Dad.'

Sophie's father, a consultant surgeon in the same Auckland hospital in which Greg worked, sniffed incredulously. Then he modified his tone. 'Even so, that doesn't mean you can never come back to live in Auckland. We have general practices up here as well.' Her father managed to make the practice of family health sound like an alternative therapy. 'Just because Greg has decided that general practice isn't for him, that certainly isn't enough of a reason for you to break off your engagement.'

'That's not the only reason.' Sophie sighed, tipped her glass upside down and then looked longingly towards the fridge. She needed a cordless telephone.

'He apparently thinks it has a lot to do with it.'

'Our engagement had become a habit, Dad. We hardly saw each other during our house-surgeon rotations and now we're going in different directions. If our relationship was strong enough for marriage it would have happened years ago. We're good friends. We always will be, but it's not enough.'

'It's what your mother and I started with. It was good enough for us.'

Sophie's memories of her mother had faded in the years since her death but she had never appeared to her daughter to be a particularly happy or fulfilled person.

'It's not enough for me,' Sophie stated bravely. 'Not any more. I've got my own life to lead, Dad. I'm making my own decisions now.'

Her father snorted with exasperation. 'You always have. You're stubborn, Sophie, and I have to say I think you're making a big mistake. Your abilities and education are being wasted.'

'And I suppose they wouldn't be wasted if I married Greg?'

'They wouldn't be wasted if you came back and took up some kind of specialist training.'

'I am doing specialist training,' Sophie snapped. 'I happen to think that general practice *is* special.' She heard a beeper sound over the phone and her father sighed heavily.

'I've got to go. We'll continue this some other time, Sophie.'

Sophie had no doubts about that. She stared at the phone as she replaced the receiver. Why had it always been so impossible to win her father's approval? And why didn't it start to matter less the more often it happened?

Greg used to approve of her. Their high-school romance had flourished as Greg had supported Sophie's attempts at independence in her choice of clothing, sports and recreation. Her father had disapproved of her staying away from home. Sophie and Greg had joined a tramping club and had gone on as many weekend expeditions as possible. Her father disliked loud music. Sophie and Greg had gone to rock and roll dancing lessons and had used the conservatory at Sophie's house to practise. The years at medical school had seen an improvement in her relationship with her father, but it had been the calm before the storm. The storm being Sophie's adamant desire to work in general practice.

Even then Greg had supported her. They both shared a vision of the satisfaction and value of being part of a community and committed to good, old-fashioned, front-line medicine. It was the perfect scenario for doctors married to each other. Even Ruby Murdock recognised that. She could share the practice and cut her hours down while the children were babies. A flexible partnership. Family and community orientated. Not driven by ambition and high-powered consultancy positions. That had been the plan right from the start. It had been their wholehearted agreement on such a lifestyle choice that had cemented their relationship to the point of announcing their engagement.

The plan had remained intact as both Sophie and Greg had moved through the range of specialties appropriate to GP training, including paediatrics, general medicine, A and E, general surgery and geriatrics. It had remained intact right up until the time they had both been due to enrol in the family medicine training programme when Greg had started his run in intensive care. Greg's change in ambitions had begun gradually but had gathered momentum. The plan hadn't been abandoned exactly. Just modified. Sophie could still be a GP, could still work part time when the children came along, but Greg would stay at the hospital. He couldn't bear to give up the excitement and challenge of dealing with the critically ill.

It had been a huge disappointment for Sophie. She'd tried to adjust. She'd thought she'd been successful. She could still be happy in general practice even if she wasn't married to her professional partner. It didn't matter that Greg's ambitions didn't quite match the person she'd thought she'd known so well. It didn't matter that he wasn't exactly like...

Like Oliver Spencer. Committed to community medicine. Caring for the people who weren't critically ill. People who sometimes needed a holistic approach to their health care. Someone who recognised the importance of his position and wasn't remotely bothered by the low ranking many specialists bestowed on general practitioners.

Damn Oliver Spencer! Sophie refilled her wine glass but then set it down on the bench beside the now wilting roses. She rubbed at the empty space on her finger created by the absence of her ring. It was definitely Oliver Spencer's fault. He was exactly what Greg was supposed to be. Or at least become. The fact that he was also a very attractive person was only a secondary consideration. Wasn't it?

Sophie groaned aloud. It couldn't be any sort of consideration now. As far as Oliver Spencer was concerned, she was getting married on July twenty-fifth. Sophie had moved herself up from the status of a happily engaged woman. Now she had stepped into the blushing bride-to-be category.

A bride-to-be whose main reason to blush might be in trying to find an explanation for her missing engagement ring.

CHAPTER THREE

IT WAS no big deal.

Sophie would simply tell the truth. Well, not quite all of it. She couldn't go as far as confessing having simply invented a fictitious wedding date. She had her story in place by the time she parked outside St David's Medical Centre on Tuesday morning.

I rang Greg to discuss the wedding arrangements, she would say, and we had a long talk. Would you believe we decided that we didn't really want to get married after all?

It bothered Sophie considerably that it would take another lie to cover up the first. Tangled webs and all that, she warned herself. She could imagine the surprise with which her colleagues would greet her news. Perhaps if she told Toni first then the news could filter through and they could all have a chat about it when she wasn't there.

Janet would look sympathetic but wise. Her romances always seemed to end in disaster. Toni would be disappointed. At thirty-three, St David's practice manager had never been married and didn't appear to have anyone special in her life, and she absolutely loved weddings and babies. There was a noticeboard in her office area plastered with photographs that the centre's patients had given her over the years. Gurgling babies and happy bridal parties. And cats. Sophie and many of their patients knew that Toni had two Burmese cats she was very fond of. They assumed she would be just as interested in their pets as in their family celebrations and additions. She was, too. Toni had a very warm personality and seemed to take great pleasure in involving herself with the lives of others. Yes, Toni would be disappointed.

Josh would probably congratulate her on her maturity. He would probably congratulate himself as well, for having dispensed such good advice which she had obviously taken to heart. And Oliver? How would Oliver react? Would the teasing which had hinted at how smitten Oliver Spencer was with his registrar cease now that the safety net of her unavailability had gone? Or would it ignite into something far more intimate? A rampant affair perhaps—or a meltdown of physical attraction that would quickly burn itself out.

Sophie had no experience of meltdowns and the thought of a short-lived affair, however incredible, wasn't attractive. It was, however, rather exciting. Sophie found she was breathing a lot harder than the walk up the ramp to the front door justified. Best not to think about Oliver Spencer's reaction or she might lose whatever courage she had finally summoned to deal with the situation.

Her arrival proved an anticlimax after all that worry. The office area behind the reception counter was somewhat chaotic. A man Sophie vaguely recognised was standing, writing busily on a clipboard. Janet was crouched on the floor, sorting the drugs, including their small supply of narcotics, to put away in the floor safe. Toni Marsh was negotiating both these obstacles as she switched her attention between the two telephones, the appointment book, the computer and the fax machine. She smiled with an it's-one-of-those-days-again expression as she continued talking into the phone.

'How old are the children, Jackie?' Toni listened for a moment. 'We don't normally give children flu vaccinations.'

Sophie glanced at the big poster in prime position opposite the front door as she walked in. 'When Autumn Skies Arrive—It's Time To Immunise.' She walked through the archway as Toni covered the mouthpiece of the phone and spoke to the man with the clipboard.

'We're getting very low on computer paper and envelopes.'

He nodded and continued scribbling as Toni uncovered the mouthpiece. 'Are the children on preventative medicine for their asthma, Jackie...? In that case...' She looked over to where Janet was still crouched, her arm through the hole in the floor as she deposited a box of drug ampoules into the safe. 'What's the new recommendation for the free vaccines, Jan?'

'Over sixty-fives and anyone with a chronic illness requiring continuous medication.'

'Asthma?'

Janet nodded. She heaved the heavy lid of the safe into place and slotted the carpet square back into position. Sophie tried to edge in to see if Toni had placed any patient files into her in-basket yet.

'The vaccinations will be free for both the children, Jackie. What time would you like to bring them in? Remember you'll have to wait for twenty minutes afterwards just in case of any adverse reactions.'

'What about paper clips?' the man asked. 'And white-out?'

Sophie wriggled the fingers of her left hand experimentally. Maybe no one would even notice. No one did. Perversely disappointed, Sophie stepped back out of the office just as the front door burst open. An elderly man was supporting a small, white-haired woman. She was deathly pale and had blood streaming down the side of her face despite the large towel the man was holding against her head.

'Mrs Benny!' Toni slammed the phone down. 'Oh, dear! What's happened?'

'She's had a bit of a fall.' Mr Benny looked almost as pale as his wife. 'Is Dr Cooper in?'

'Not yet.' Sophie already had her arm around the woman. Janet took over holding the dressing. 'But we'll look after you.' She nodded at Janet. 'Let's take Mrs Benny into the treatment room so she can lie down.'

'It was such a silly thing.' Mrs Benny sounded very shaky. 'I was feeding the cat and I dropped some of the jellymeat. When I stood on it, I slipped.'

'She caught the corner of the table as she went down,' Mr Benny growled anxiously. 'Bloody cat!'

'It wasn't Tabitha's fault, dear.'

They covered their patient with a warm blanket. Sophie and Janet both donned gloves quickly and Sophie inspected the head wound.

'It's not too bad,' she reported with relief. 'Scalp lacerations can bleed badly. It's going to need a couple of stitches, though. Were you knocked unconscious at all, Mrs Benny?'

'No. But my wrist hurts, dear. And my knee.'

Sophie took the gauze dressing that Janet had moistened with saline and pressed it into place on the scalp wound. 'Hold this,' she directed Janet, 'while I have a look at that wrist.' Bent up at an awkward angle, Sophie was already confident there was a fracture that needed splinting. Mrs Benny's knee was also going to need looking at and her patient was worryingly pale. Taking her blood pressure was a priority. Did she have a cardiac history at all? Sophie's thoughts raced. Janet was peering anxiously at Mrs Benny's face as she pressed on the dressing to control the bleeding from the scalp laceration. Toni was hovering in the doorway, looking even more anxious.

'Should I call an ambulance?' she queried.

'Not yet.' The calm tone of Oliver Spencer's voice sent a wave of relief through Sophie. Oliver dropped his briefcase and jacket and unbuttoned his shirtsleeves. He had rolled them up by the time he reached the bed and took hold of Mrs Benny's wrist.

'What have you been up to, Muriel?' he asked with concern. 'You seem to have given everyone a bit of a fright.' He glanced at Sophie. 'Let's have some oxygen and get a blood pressure.'

Sophie moved quickly. She could think clearly again. Oliver's presence had negated the escalating anxiety levels in the room. Even Mr Benny had visibly relaxed.

'How does your chest feel at the moment, Muriel? This hasn't brought your angina on, has it? Any pain or tightness at all?'

'I don't think so.' Muriel Benny smiled shakily. Sophie slipped the oxygen mask in place and tightened the elastic band.

'Put the monitor on after you've got a blood pressure,' Oliver directed Sophie. He lifted the dressing. 'Janet, can you set up a suture tray and get me some gloves, please?'

Sophie finally stripped off her own gloves as she left the room twenty minutes later to arrange ambulance transfer to the hospital for Mrs Benny. Oliver had completed suturing the laceration and Sophie had splinted the broken wrist and bandaged their patient's bruised and swollen knee. Now she needed X-rays and treatment they could not provide at St David's.

Oliver had coped with the dramatic and disruptive start to the morning surgery hours with no apparent annoyance but he was looking irritated by the time he joined Sophie in the main office. He sighed at the sight of the crowded waiting room, smiled briefly at Toni and then frowned as his gaze raked Sophie. Turning away abruptly, he snatched up the first file in his in-basket and barked out the patient's name. A middle-aged woman flung her magazine hurriedly onto the coffee-table as she rose. It slithered to the floor and she turned to retrieve it. Oliver tapped the file against his leg impatiently and stared at Sophie, still sitting beside the phone.

'Where's your ring, then?' he demanded. 'Oh, I suppose you've sent it away to have a matching wedding ring made.'

'No.' Sophie's denial was a trifle hesitant. She hadn't thought of anyone putting that interpretation on her action. Why did Oliver seem so annoyed with her? Had she done something wrong when assisting him with Mrs Benny?

Oliver's lip curled fractionally. 'Don't tell me you've changed your mind since yesterday.'

'No, of course not.' Sophie's prepared escape route vanished in the face of Oliver's accusatory tone, mingled with the worry she now felt that her treatment

of Mrs Benny might not have been up to scratch. 'I...
The stone was loose. I've got to get it fixed.'

Oliver's frown deepened and Sophie cursed the
tell-tale flush she could feel creeping up her neck. Did
he know she was lying? Oliver shrugged, a small
movement that advertised—what? That it was of no
importance? He gestured with the file he held. 'This
way, Colleen. Sorry to have kept you waiting. We
had a bit of an emergency.'

'That's quite all right, Dr Spencer.' Colleen
sounded unperturbed. 'I don't mind waiting to see
you.'

Fifteen minutes later Sophie was again in the reception area, having just seen the Bennys off. They
were both looking much happier and Mrs Benny
wasn't showing any signs of concussion. Misgivings
about her own performance during the emergency had
faded as she'd given a cheerful wave to the ambulance driver. Sophie had still been smiling as she
headed back inside. Her smile faded rapidly. She
could hear the sound of the raised voice even before
she opened the front door. The patients sitting in the
waiting room were staring with open fascination at
the scene. Even Toni was looking flustered as Oliver's
patient, Colleen, jabbed at the slip of paper on the
counter before her and continued her tirade.

'I'm not paying this. And I do not want to see Dr
Spencer again. I'll have another appointment, thank
you!' The woman's chest heaved with indignation.
'He accused me of lying to him. It's quite outra-
geous!'

'When did you want to make another appointment
for, Miss Thompson?'

'I don't think I want to make one at all. Not at *this*

medical centre.' Colleen Thompson threw a pitying glance around the waiting room. Everyone instantly dropped their gazes back to their magazines. Colleen sniffed loudly. 'And I'm *not* paying this account.'

Sophie didn't stop after she'd gone through the archway. She carried on to the end of the corridor and into the staffroom where she found Oliver drinking a glass of water.

'Not a happy customer, then,' she observed lightly.

Oliver shrugged. 'Can't win 'em all, I suppose.'

'You usually do,' Sophie ventured.

'Well, maybe this time I can't be bothered.'

Sophie's jaw dropped a fraction. This was a side to Oliver Spencer she had never encountered. 'She's a difficult patient, I take it?'

Oliver snorted. 'She's overweight, asthmatic, is getting increasing angina and is non-compliant with medications. She also refuses to try and give up smoking.'

'Oh.' Sophie looked at the set of Oliver's jaw. He was obviously livid.

'That's not the problem, however,' Oliver said fiercely. 'The problem is that she won't tell the truth. How can you relate to anybody who's prepared to tell blatant lies to your face?'

Sophie said nothing. Her finger had never felt so naked. She could feel a return of that guilty flush but Oliver wasn't even looking at her. He deposited his empty glass on the bench with a thud.

'She sat there, *reeking* of cigarette smoke, and swore black and blue that she hasn't touched them for over a month. When I made even the mildest suggestion that she might not be being entirely truthful with me, she hit the roof. Knocked over her handbag

and simply ignored the fact that her packet of ciga-
rettes and lighter fell out. She told me it wasn't her
fault she wasn't getting well. Her health was my responsibility and I obviously wasn't good enough at
my job.' Oliver shook his head angrily. 'I couldn't
get a word in edgeways. Next thing I know, she's
stormed off and is busy informing everyone about
what an inadequate doctor I am.'

'She sounds totally impossible,' Sophie sympathised. 'Let's hope she does take her business elsewhere
as she threatened Toni she would.'

'She will. She's been through ten GPs in as many
years.' Oliver still sounded angry. 'I thought I was
getting somewhere, you know? I've spent months
supporting her with her smoking cessation programme and diet and exercise regimes. What a bloody
waste of time.' Oliver stalked off. 'I don't know why
I bother with some people.'

Sophie eyed his retreating figure. He wouldn't want
to bother with her either, if he discovered her own
blatant lying to his face. She sighed deeply. The
smooth camaraderie of St David's seemed to be off
the rails and she couldn't help feeling it was a ripple
effect from the disruption to her own life. Perhaps if
she kept her head down things might begin to settle
a bit by lunchtime.

Oliver's mood, however, didn't seem to have im-
proved to any noticeable degree by lunchtime, despite
the exotic contribution to their meals provided by the
visiting drug company representative, Christine
Prescott. When Sophie finally returned to the staffroom for a quick break, Oliver was staring rather mo-
rosely at a platter of sushi on the dining table.

'This is just a quick social visit,' Christine explained, having greeted Sophie enthusiastically. 'It seems far too long since I was in Christchurch and St David's is absolutely my favourite medical centre.' She beamed at Oliver and then nodded approvingly at Josh who was eagerly reaching for another sushi roll.

'This is fantastic,' Josh said happily. 'All we need is a nice little Jacobs Creek Riesling to chase it with.'

Sophie eyed the platter suspiciously. 'That green stuff on the outside is seaweed, right?'

'Try some,' Josh urged. 'You're such an unadventurous lot.' He cast a disapproving look at Oliver. 'You haven't even tasted it and Christine went to a lot of trouble to find something interesting. It's not often we get treated like this at work.'

'Did I give you one of these, Sophie?' The drug rep pushed a small, black, zipped case across the table.

Sophie put it beside the stack of ballpoint pens and the mouse pad with Christine's drug company logo and advertising for drugs on them. The black case sported similar adornments. Sophie had only met Christine once before but visits to the medical centre by other drug reps were frequent enough to be something of a nuisance. Toni was becoming selective over who was allowed access to the doctors. They always came bearing gifts, food and exciting news of whatever pharmaceuticals their company was currently promoting in the hope that they might become a mainstay of the centre's prescribing habits. Sophie suspected that each company must have an entire department concentrating on coming up with ideas for attention-grabbing trinkets. The small black case contained a miniature set of boules, no bigger than golf balls, the jack the size of a marble.

'You can put a little sand box on your desk,' Oliver suggested dryly, watching as Sophie inspected the contents of the case. 'Then you can play with them when you get a boring patient.'

Christine laughed. 'They do come up with some great ideas, don't they? I've got a huge carton of these in the car. I'm supposed to get around every Christchurch practice in the next three days.' She sighed and shook the mane of luxuriant blonde hair that framed her vivacious face. She reached delicately for a sushi roll and dipped it expertly in the Wasabi sauce. 'It's a tough job.' She smiled. 'But somebody's gotta do it.'

Sophie exchanged a glance with Toni and they both smiled. Drug reps were, by and large, a very attractive group of young women with outgoing and confident personalities. Christine Prescott was a top-of-the-line example. A bit over the top, in fact, especially that big hair. Sophie's head felt quite naked in comparison. As naked as her finger.

Oliver pushed back his chair. 'Speaking of tough jobs,' he said crisply, 'it's time I got on with mine.' He nodded at Christine without smiling. 'Thanks for the samples but I doubt that I'll change the beta blocker I currently prescribe. Cheaper is not necessarily better.' He walked off abruptly, leaving Christine looking disconcerted again.

'Don't worry,' Josh reassured her. He also looked a little taken aback by Oliver's unusual discourtesy. 'Someone's rattled his cage a bit, I expect. No reflection on you.'

'Maybe it was the sushi.' Christine was recovering

fast. 'I'll have to try and find something Oliver will really like next time.' She was staring thoughtfully at the door Oliver had left open.

'Muffins,' Toni suggested. 'Or, better yet, something really basic like peanut brownies or chocolate-chip cookies. Our Oliver likes good, old-fashioned, honest food.'

Sophie zipped up the black case slowly. Oliver liked everything—and everyone—good and honest. No wonder his cage had been rattled by his patient's behaviour. If he knew what she herself was guilty of… She transferred her gaze to Toni who was nibbling experimentally on a sushi roll.

'I quite like it.' Toni sounded surprised.

'That's great. Enjoy the rest. I'll have to go.' Christine excused herself. 'I'll see you in a few weeks when I'm back in town.' She reached for her coat. 'Back out into the cold.'

Sophie exchanged another quick glance with Toni. Christine's miniskirt would probably have given her chilly legs no matter what the season. Sophie and Toni both dressed neatly for work but their skirts and tops were conservative by comparison with the young drug rep's wardrobe.

'I'll see you out.' Josh was on his feet fast enough to help Christine with her coat. He then held the door open and Christine's smile indicated that his courtesy was more than making up for his junior partner's earlier brusqueness.

Sophie grinned. 'He's the perfect gentleman, isn't he?'

Toni had an odd expression on her face. 'Oh, yes,' she agreed quietly. 'As long as the subject is worthy.'

She took her glasses off and began to polish the lenses with a tissue.

'How did your visit with the optometrist go?'

Toni brightened considerably. 'We talked about laser surgery again. I've always been put off because the results for higher degrees of myopia aren't so good, but there's a new technique now.'

'Really? What's that?'

'LASIK. Commonly known as "flap and zap".' Toni pushed her spectacles back into place and picked up one of the pens beside Sophie. Turning over one of the broadsheets Christine had left on the table, she rapidly drew a circular diagram on it.

'You know how shortsightedness is caused by the eye being too long and the cornea too curved so that the light is focused in front of the retina.' Toni was illustrating her point with rapid additions to her diagram.

Sophie nodded. 'The laser is used to flatten the cornea and redirect the light, isn't it?'

'Yes.' Toni coloured in the front portion of the eye she had drawn. 'But when a greater degree of correction is needed it can leave problems with scarring and corneal haze. You can even end up with a worse refraction error than you started with.'

'A bit offputting.'

'With flap and zap, they take a layer off the whole cornea first and roll it up to one side. It's only three times the thickness of a human hair. Then they reshape the central five millimetres of the cornea. It's all computer controlled and very accurate. Then the flap goes back. It's improving the outcome and cutting down on a lot of the complications.'

'Are you going to try it, then?' Sophie was intrigued by Toni's knowledge and enthusiasm. The diagrams she had drawn were impressively clear. Sophie would have to copy the design when she wanted to explain visual problems to her patients.

'I'm going to get my first eye done on Friday,' Toni told her. 'They only use local anaesthetic drops and with this technique you can be back at work in one to two days instead of a week. I'll have the weekend to recover.'

'Is it expensive?'

'Mmm.' Toni shrugged. 'But what else do I have to spend my money on? They'll only do one eye at a time, but if it goes well I'll have the other one done in a couple of months. I might even be able to throw my glasses away.'

'Let me know if I can help at all,' Sophie offered. 'If you need a lift anywhere or anything.'

'I'll be fine,' Toni assured her. 'I've got it all worked out. Don't tell Josh or Oliver, though.'

'Why not?'

'They might try and talk me out of it. Josh might be worried that I'll need too much time off work.'

'Or he might try convincing you how intelligent you look wearing glasses and you shouldn't give them up.'

Toni groaned. 'I look like a secretary. Or a librarian. Efficient and boring.'

'Never.' Sophie smiled warmly at her colleague. 'And what's more, you're a lot braver than me. You even ate the sushi.'

Toni eyed the remains of the food. 'That sauce was a bit fiery. Maybe Janet will like it. I'd better get back to the office and let her have some lunch.'

'Let's hope the afternoon doesn't produce any

more dissatisfied customers.' Sophie carried her coffee-mug to the sink. 'You really got an earful this morning.'

'Water off a duck's back,' Toni said cheerfully. 'I think Oliver took it to heart, though. He didn't look too happy.'

Oliver Spencer still didn't look too happy on Wednesday morning but Sophie managed to keep out of his way until lunchtime. She could hear him talking to Josh in the staffroom as she walked down the hallway.

'Great legs! She's perfect for you, Oliver.'

Sophie glanced down at the skirt she was wearing. She couldn't see much of her legs. She knew they weren't overly chunky and they did their part to contribute to her height of five feet five, but she would never have described them as great.

'I suppose I should apologise,' Oliver responded to Josh. 'I was a bit rude yesterday.'

'That would be a good start.' Josh was nodding approvingly as Sophie entered the room. Oliver got to his feet hurriedly.

'I've got a house call to make,' he excused himself. 'See you later.'

'What's Oliver making a good start on?' Sophie asked curiously. 'He didn't look very enthusiastic.'

'He will.' Josh grinned. 'I'm just giving him a push in Christine Prescott's direction. Might stop him pining over you.'

Sophie was saved having to think up a suitable response by Toni's abrupt entrance.

'Deborah McQueen just rang, Josh.'

'Oh, no!' Josh made a pained face. 'I knew there was something about today I'd forgotten to tell you.'

He looked at his watch and groaned. 'Was she furious?'

'I explained that you had an unavoidable emergency and would be with her as soon as possible,' Toni said primly. 'I also suggested that it was merely one of the downsides of a relationship with a doctor and that even important lunch dates had to take second place to patients.' Toni was almost smiling. 'I suggested she had another cappuccino while she waited.'

'You're a life-saver, Swampy. I'll be back in an hour.' Josh was already halfway through the door again. 'I owe you one.'

'You owe me a hell of a lot more than one,' Toni responded wryly.

'Who's Deborah McQueen?' Sophie enquired as she followed Toni back to the front desk.

'Oh, just the feminine flavour of the month,' Toni told her casually. 'She won't last. In fact, if she's half as rude to him about being kept waiting for lunch as she was to me, I'd say we probably won't hear from her again.'

'Where does he find them all?' Sophie wondered aloud.

'They find him,' Toni muttered darkly. 'And some of them don't want to disappear. He has a sort of fly paper sexual attraction.'

'He is pretty attractive,' Sophie conceded.

'You don't mean…?' Toni looked vaguely alarmed.

'Heavens, no!' Sophie laughed. 'He's not my type at all. Besides…' Sophie was unable to finish her sentence. She couldn't voice another blatant lie about being a happily engaged woman. She cleared her throat. 'Oliver seems a bit more restrained in that direction.'

Toni nodded, her face relaxing. 'There's been the occasional woman over the last few years but nothing serious. I think his divorce put him off.'

'Did you know his wife?'

'No, the marriage was over well before he came to St David's. From what I've gathered, it didn't last very long anyway. Short and not sweet. Oliver's never said much but Josh once held him up as a shining example of what damage marrying the wrong person could do. A situation our Josh would never contemplate risking.' Toni shook her head a little wearily but then smiled at Sophie. 'I got some sandwiches for you when I popped down to the bank. Have you got time before you head off for your tutorial at the hospital?'

Sophie glanced at the wall clock, repressing her curiosity to know why Oliver's marriage had been such a disaster. How could any woman not be happy, being married to Oliver and having his undivided attention? Maybe the attention hadn't been undivided. Sophie collected her errant thoughts quickly. 'I've got half an hour. I'll come and get the sandwiches when I've sorted out what I need to take. Thanks, Toni— you really look after us all. Are you having lunch?'

'Sure am. It's finally calmed down around here and no one's due for another hour. We'll finally get to have that chat. I *still* have no idea what your wedding dress will look like.'

You and me both, Sophie thought with dismay. Maybe lunch wasn't such a good idea. It took only a minute to collect her white coat and check her supply of pens and notepaper. When she returned to the front desk she found Toni talking to someone else.

'I'm afraid Dr Spencer has been called out to visit a patient. He won't be back for some time. And Dr Cooper is out. He isn't starting his afternoon clinic until 2 p.m. Both the doctors are fully booked in any case. We could fit you in tomorrow morning.' Toni flipped the pages of the appointment book. 'Or is it something that our practice nurse, Janet, might be able to help you with?'

'No.' The woman looked tired. Sophie moved to collect the packet of sandwiches Toni had put aside for her, glancing into the reception area as she did so. The woman walked over to where her toddler was emptying the toy basket. 'It doesn't really matter,' she said quietly.

Sophie sensed that something mattered rather a lot. 'I have some time now, Toni,' she murmured. 'If it would help.'

Toni glanced pointedly at the wrapped sandwiches. Sophie shrugged. 'I can eat in the car.' She smiled and Toni nodded, turning back to the woman.

'Would you like to see our GP registrar, Dr Bennett, Mrs King?'

'Oh, yes—please. My mother thinks she's wonderful.'

Sophie ducked her head modestly at the grin which accompanied Toni's raised eyebrows.

'Leave Laura out here if you like,' Toni suggested. 'I'll keep an eye on her.' She tapped an entry into the computer, glanced at the patient number and moved with unerring accuracy to extract a file from the huge shelf that covered the end wall.

Sophie took it on her way out. 'Come with me,

Mrs King.' She looked down at the file. Felicity King. 'Oh!' she exclaimed. 'Are you Mrs Murdock's daughter?'

'That's right. I've been hearing wonderful things about you, Dr Bennett.'

Sophie laughed. 'Not half as wonderful as what I hear about you, I'm sure.' She ushered Felicity King into her consulting room. 'Please, sit down and tell me how I can help,' she invited.

Felicity sat down with a heavy sigh. 'I think I might be pregnant,' she said flatly.

It was clearly not a welcome possibility. 'What makes you think you might be, Mrs King?'

'Felicity,' her patient corrected. 'I've missed my period. That's never happened before except when I was pregnant.'

'Any other signs?'

'No.'

'Have you done a home test or anything?'

'No. I was putting it off. I really couldn't cope if it was bad news.'

'Well, the first thing to do is to test you. We can do that right now if you can give us a small urine specimen.'

Felicity nodded wearily. Sophie looked at her thoughtfully. The mental image she'd had of Ruby Murdock's extraordinary daughter, who dashed about and looked so much younger than her thirty-four years, did not match the woman before her. There was more to this visit than worry about a possible pregnancy.

'You have three children, don't you, Felicity?'

Her patient nodded.

'And you do a lot for your mother. It's a lot to cope with, isn't it?'

Felicity King looked at Sophie, her eyes rapidly filling with tears. 'I can't cope any more. I really can't... And I don't know what to do.' With that, Felicity King—Super daughter—burst into a fit of distraught sobbing.

Sophie passed tissues and waited for the storm to subside a little. 'Would you like to tell me about it, Felicity?' she suggested gently. 'Maybe I can help.'

It was a long story. Sophie heard about what a wonderful mother and grandmother Ruby had been. How Felicity had relied on her help when the boys were small.

'Even after Dad died, she coped. She couldn't do enough for us, really. Babysitting, cleaning, cooking and so on. And then she broke her ankle. She tripped over Nathan's bike. I felt like it was all my fault.'

'So you began helping your mother instead of her helping you?'

'It was the least I could do, and it was only going to be until she got back on her feet again. But she never did, not really. She seemed to lose interest in the children and put on all that weight. I started out just helping with the cleaning once a week, but when she broke her wrist I started cooking her meals.'

Sophie raised her eyebrows. 'All of them?'

'Oh, no. Only dinners.'

'This would have been about the time your mother's asthma started.'

'Yes.' Felicity blew her nose and then sniffed. 'That's when I started doing her shopping with her. I've tried to cut down—not do as many meals and things—but she gets upset and her asthma gets worse. I'm trapped.'

'You're *still* doing all her meals?'

Felicity nodded miserably. 'I've tried just to cook extra at home and take her some of that, but it's not good enough. She never says anything but if she likes her dinner she washes the plate. If she doesn't like it, it's sitting there on the bench for me the next day with all the food poked around and left.'

Sophie's assessment of Ruby Murdock's personality slipped a notch.

'She won't eat rice. She's got false teeth and says the bits get stuck. She won't eat salad or pasta or anything easy. It has to be meat and three veg. And something different every day. It's hard enough trying to think of what to feed Brent and the children, let alone Mum.'

'How does Brent feel about your extra workload?'

'He doesn't get on with Mum any more. In fact, our marriage isn't so great just now. It'll be the last straw if I'm pregnant. He didn't even want us to have three children and he had a vasectomy when I was pregnant with Laura, but they don't always work, do they?'

'Let's find out.' Sophie stood up and collected a specimen jar from her cupboard. 'And then we'll have a think about what to do to reduce a bit of your stress. There's lots of help your mother can get. Home help and meals on wheels and so on. It doesn't all have to fall on your shoulders, you know.'

'I've never thought of asking for help before. Especially not from a doctor. It's not as if I'm sick or anything. I only came in for a pregnancy test.'

'Well, it's a good thing you did,' Sophie said

firmly. 'Sometimes asking for help is the most difficult part, and a doctor is a good person to start with no matter what the problem is. It's what we're here for. If we can't help you ourselves, then we'll know someone who can.'

Felicity King smiled for the first time as she accepted the specimen jar from Sophie. 'Thanks. I almost feel as if I can cope with this now. Whatever the result.'

'It was a negative result. She isn't pregnant.'

Sophie was sitting in the staffroom, having returned to St David's after the lengthy afternoon workshop in order to write up her notes on the consultation with Felicity King. By the time she finished it was 6 p.m. and Sophie was surprised to find Oliver in the staffroom. The other staff members had gone home. Curious to know whether Oliver's unusual mood had worn off, Sophie busied herself making a cup of coffee, and telling Oliver about the unexpected visit as she did so.

She sat at the table and put her mug down carefully. 'It's funny, isn't it? I thought Ruby Murdock was a sweet, motherly type. Seems like she's manipulating her poor daughter into a serious depression.'

'Hmm.' Oliver looked thoughtful. 'I've only ever treated the children since Laura was born. Felicity's never hinted at any problems.' He smiled at Sophie. 'Perhaps it needed the feminine touch.'

'Or maybe the pregnancy scare was the last straw.' Sophie returned the smile with relief. This was more like the Oliver she knew. As she relaxed she uncurled the tight fist her left hand made. The movement made her draw her breath in sharply.

'What's up?' Oliver's eyebrows shot up in concern.

'Oh, nothing.' Sophie felt embarrassed. She looked down at her left hand and the wad of tissue still clutched in it. Oliver followed the line of her gaze.

'What the hell...?' He was on his feet in a fluid movement. Two steps brought him to the table. His hand curled around Sophie's wrist as he lifted her hand. The bloodstained tissues rolled off her palm.

'It's just a little nick,' Sophie said hurriedly. 'My own stupidity. The skin on those lumps of pork we were practising on were a lot tougher than they looked. I got a bit carried away.' She laughed a little too loudly. 'Perhaps I shouldn't be allowed to wield a scalpel, unsupervised, after all.'

Oliver didn't appear to be listening. He still held her wrist captive with one hand. With the other he was examining the cut on the underside of her ring finger.

'Right,' he said finally. 'You're coming with me.'

'What?' Sophie scrambled to her feet. She had no choice. Oliver was still holding her wrist like a human handcuff and he was already moving towards the door. 'It's quite clean. I was just waiting for the bleeding to stop completely. Then I'll put a sticking plaster on it.'

'It needs stitching,' Oliver stated. 'Or at least some steri-strips.'

'I can do that,' Sophie protested. They were entering the treatment room. 'Really, there's no need for you to—'

'How are you going to manage that?' Oliver stopped and Sophie found his face only inches from her own. There was a renewed hint of anger in his expression. 'Hold one end with your teeth?'

Sophie made no further protest. She sat meekly as Oliver cleaned and dried the wound. The steri-strips were positioned carefully, drawing the edges of skin together closely enough to heal neatly. Then he put a dressing on top and wound a thin gauze bandage along the length of her finger.

'You'll have to keep it dry for a few days,' he said crisply. 'And the steri-strips will need to stay on for at least a week.'

'OK. Thanks, Oliver.' Sophie was ready to slide off the bed she was sitting on but Oliver was still standing too close. His thigh was touching her knees.

'Rather a shame,' Oliver added.

'Mmm. I never thought I was that clumsy.'

'That wasn't what I meant.' Oliver still didn't move away. 'I meant that it's a shame it's that particular finger. Even when you get your ring fixed you won't be able to wear it for a while. A couple of weeks at least, I should imagine.'

'I'm not worried,' Sophie said quickly. She did *not* want to discuss her ring. 'It's no big deal.'

'Isn't it?' Oliver managed to give his query an inflection that implied he was talking about far more than a piece of jewellery. Sophie swallowed with some difficulty.

'I've always thought an engagement was quite a sizeable deal,' Oliver continued calmly. 'But maybe if I'd had one as long as yours I might have got rather complacent about it as well.'

'I'm not complacent. Just…'

'Confident?'

'I suppose.' Sophie gave a wriggle to advertise her desire to get off the bed. Oliver failed to take the hint and Sophie now found her knees pressed firmly against his leg. She caught his eye and then wished she hadn't. The intensity was unnerving.

'Josh could be right, you know.'

'Really?' The sensations that seemed to be drawn from Oliver's leg into her own body were fascinating. Sophie could feel them spreading, lodging in the pit of her stomach and tightening her chest wall.

'Maybe you can't be completely confident without some form of comparison.'

The eye contact was locked on. Sophie couldn't have escaped even if she'd wanted to. And she didn't want to. But this was dangerous territory, the closest Sophie had come to real danger that she could think of. And she didn't even want to step back. She cleared her throat nervously.

'Who...who exactly did you have in mind?'

Oliver smiled. A lazy, slow smile that was almost predatory. Sophie felt a flash of real fear as his lips brushed hers lightly. Then they settled more firmly and the fear was banished by a far more electrifying sensation. She could feel that kiss with every nerve in her entire body. Sophie closed her eyes and opened her mouth, dissolving into the sensation as she felt Oliver's hands cradle her head, tilting it far enough to deepen the kiss. Sophie had no control whatsoever. Oliver was exploring her mouth...tasting her soul. The intimacy was shocking but Sophie had no desire to even try and pull away. Her hands touched Oliver's chest and were about to slide up across the ridge of hard muscle towards his neck when Oliver finally released his hold on Sophie's mouth.

'Does Greg kiss you like that?' Oliver asked softly.

Sophie gasped. How could Oliver even think about Greg when that kiss had made her feel as if they were the only two humans in existence? Had his only intention been to provoke and unsettle her?

'What are you trying to do?' Sophie whispered in bewilderment. How could Oliver have the power to make her feel the way he just had and then use that power to manipulate her so casually? Had she been entirely wrong in her assessment of Oliver Spencer's integrity?

Oliver seemed taken aback by her reaction. His face creased placatingly. 'Look, it was just a kiss. Nothing to get so worked up about. You're not married yet and I'm not proposing that we ride off into the sunset together or anything.' His lips quirked into a smile. 'I was just supplying a basis for comparison. It seemed like a good way of letting you know I'd be a more than willing candidate. What do you think?'

The wave of disappointment was crushing. So that was all that Oliver was offering. A quick fling with him to see if Greg really made the grade? A legitimate excuse for a happily engaged woman to do a bit of bed-hopping? Oliver Spencer clearly gave no thought to how it might affect anyone else. He was quite prepared to let Sophie hurt her supposed fiancé by being unfaithful so he didn't give a damn about Greg's feelings. If she *was* happily engaged then he would be hurting Sophie at the same time. Did that mean he had no regard for her feelings as well?

Sophie found her bewilderment fading. She felt the raw endings her nerves had been left crystallising into anger.

'Is that what happened to your marriage, Oliver?' she queried coldly. 'Did your wife not stand up to the comparisons you tried?'

Oliver's face tightened enough for Sophie to see

that her accusation had hit home. 'My wife was never honest with me,' he stated deliberately. 'She lied about anything and everything.' He snorted softly. 'I never knew. She was so good at lying I didn't find out until she ran off with the man whose baby she was carrying.'

So it hadn't been Oliver's fault that his marriage had failed. That figured. She shouldn't have suggested it had been, but she still felt far too angry to apologise. She met the direct gaze with more courage than she felt. 'I would think that would give you a very good idea of how important faithfulness is in a relationship. And yet here you are, suggesting that I—'

'What it did,' Oliver cut in quietly, 'was teach me how important honesty is in a relationship.'

'Exactly,' Sophie agreed swiftly. 'But you think I should—'

Oliver interrupted again. His voice was still quiet. Almost menacing. 'I think you might be being a little less than honest, Sophie Bennett.' He took a deep breath as he turned away from her. 'Less than honest to me, less than honest to your fiancé and—perhaps more importantly—less than honest to yourself.' He gave her one last glance. 'Think about it.'

CHAPTER FOUR

SOPHIE did think about it.

On Thursday morning she was still furious at Oliver's apparent disregard for her feelings. His...arrogance, that was the only word for it. The man calmly assumed that a kiss from him—an uninvited kiss for that matter—would surpass any experience Sophie had ever had. She had no intention of giving him the satisfaction of knowing how correct his assumption had been. Let him make just one flirtatious remark and she was ready to take Oliver Spencer down a peg or two.

The opportunity didn't arise. The day was a busy one and Dr Spencer seemed intent on presenting a purely professional and carefully constrained façade. Not that anybody else would have noticed a change. It was only Sophie who could be aware that their eye contact was abruptly curtailed and that the cheerful smile seemed to come from behind a clear barrier that filtered out any real warmth. Sophie felt she was being treated like some badly behaved child. She was being punished, very subtly, by a disapproving parent. God! The last thing she needed was another father figure.

Precisely what was she being punished for? she wondered. His suspicion that she wasn't being honest? Or her lack of willingness for not wanting to leap into bed with him whilst—as far as he knew—she was engaged to another man? Maybe he was simply offended that she had turned down the invitation to explore the further delights that the kiss had so convincingly promised. Underneath all that charm Oliver Spencer was probably just like all the rest. Men were all the same. They were only interested in sex.

Maybe *that* was the problem.

By Friday Sophie's anger at Oliver's uninvited assault on her physical senses had given way to shame that she hadn't wanted him to stop. She was just as bad as he was. Another sleepless night gave her a satisfactory explanation of it all. It had to be due to the relentless workload of medical school and housesurgeon rotations, coupled with the fact that she had made a commitment to someone she'd had little time to be with. Sophie had simply been unaware of a physical requirement her body craved. The change in lifestyle and the unexpected compatibility with a colleague had released hormones she was ill equipped to deal with. Hormones that were turning her brain to mush and convincing her that she could be in love with an arrogant brute like Oliver Spencer.

Greg had never been like that. There had been no question of any meltdowns in their physical relationship. Was that why it had seemed more real? More likely to stay the distance? OK, so it had never been earth-shattering, but it had been...nice. Companionable. Comforting. Like their friendship. A friendship that could never be the same and one that Sophie was missing very badly by Monday morning.

Sophie Bennett felt more alone than she ever had. Cast adrift with nothing substantial to aim towards. Her whole life had been aimed towards the future she had mapped out so clearly. Now that was gone and she had eliminated it by her own choice. Had she

given enough thought to dealing with the conse-
quences? Sophie hadn't expected this aftershock of
guilt and grief over the termination of her engagement. Had Oliver's kiss been enough to release that
as well? Had she tipped her whole life upside down
purely because of sex?

How could she possibly have imagined that she
was in love with Oliver Spencer? It was just as well
he'd stepped behind his invisible barrier. Sophie was
in no mood to deal with even another verbal advance.
She marched into the medical centre first thing on
Monday decidedly out of sorts.

Toni's enthusiastic greeting might have helped if it
hadn't been for the huge stack of magazines she ex-
citedly handed over to Sophie.

'There are so many articles on weddings and some
of the most gorgeous dresses you've ever seen.' The
plastic shopping bag Toni presented her with was remarkably heavy. 'If you haven't already finalised all
the details, they'll give you some wonderful ideas.'

'Thanks, Toni. You shouldn't have gone to so
much trouble.'

Toni gave a dismissive wave at the bag. 'No trouble at all. I was stuck in an armchair all weekend,
resting, and I needed to sort out the magazine rack.
It took my mind off my eye very nicely, imagining
your wedding.'

Sophie grasped the new conversational direction
eagerly. 'How was the surgery?'

'A bit scary, but it didn't take that long and the
surgeon was very pleased. The pain's virtually gone
now. I'll be able to take this eye patch off in a day
or two.'

Josh looked very concerned as he arrived for work. 'Toni! What have you done to yourself?'

'Just a bit of corrective laser treatment,' Toni said breezily. 'I decided it was time for some repair work while I'm still young enough not to need reading glasses.'

Josh frowned. 'Why didn't you talk to me about it first? Have you been properly informed about possible risks? Who did the procedure? You should have checked with me about their qualifications. Your eyes are too important to meddle with lightly, you know.'

'I make my own decisions, Josh.' Toni sounded unusually sharp. 'It's my life and I intend to make the most of it. Just like you do with yours,' she added defiantly.

Josh took a step back and saluted. Then he grinned. 'I quite like the look,' he decided aloud. 'Yo, ho, ho and a bottle of rum. Where's the parrot?'

'Go away,' Toni ordered. 'Go and get on with some work.'

Sophie responded to the direction as well. She dumped the bag of magazines under her desk just as one of the handles gave way with the strain. She shoved the bag further out of sight with her foot. Looking at pictures of wedding gowns and articles on the perfect make-up for the big day, was the last thing she wanted.

It didn't help that Ruby Murdock was Sophie's first patient for the day either. She slapped the file onto the desk top and then ignored it as she stared out of the window. It *still* hadn't stopped raining. The weather over the weekend had probably been a contributing factor to how down she was feeling this morning. The glorious April weather of calm, sunny days, which were typical of Christchurch, had been obliterated by a wicked southerly blast. The torrential rain, sleet and bitter temperatures had kept Sophie cooped up in the small house she rented on the hills only a mile or so from St David's.

The house was old. The view of the Heathcote River and the character of the house had charmed Sophie when she'd seen it at the height of summer. Now it felt damp and cold, and the fact that she had completely forgotten to order in a supply of firewood became a major omission. The weather wasn't the real problem, however. Nor was the house. Or even the magazines. Sophie knew quite well that the real problem was inside herself. She was lonely.

Her consulting room was already quite tidy but Sophie fussed around. Ruby Murdock's file lay in splendid isolation in the centre of her desk. She moved the ballpoint pen a little closer and then lined up her prescription pad beside that.

It would be nice, she mused, to be able to talk to someone about it. This unexpected grief at the termination of her engagement. Greg would understand. He might even be feeling the same way. No. Sophie flipped her white coat off the back of her chair and shoved her arms into the sleeves. She had tried to ring him on Saturday evening at 8 o'clock. And at 10 and even at 11.30. Deciding that he was probably on call, she had waited and tried again on Sunday evening, with no more success than before.

All she had wanted had been some sort of reassurance that their friendship was still intact. That there was at least one person who would understand and sympathise with her. If Greg was feeling lonely he was clearly following a much more aggressive plan in dealing with it. Good on him, she had decided, trying to feel sincere in her appraisal, but it didn't quite suppress the resentment the abortive phone calls had produced.

Sophie pulled a peak-flow meter and a clean mouthpiece from her desk drawer and positioned it beside the prescription pad. The tick of the wall clock caught her attention and Sophie sighed. Maybe a quick coffee would restore her usual enthusiasm for her job.

Josh was in the staffroom. He was staring into the specimen fridge.

'Hi, Sophie.' His smile was cheerful. 'Do you have any idea what this thing is in the jam jar?'

'It came in with Mr Collins. I think Oliver is the person to ask.' She braved a look over his shoulder. 'Yuck!'

They both eyed the shrivelled brown item lying on the bottom of the glass jar. It appeared to have some kind of mould forming around its edges.

'Perhaps Mr Collins has a genuine problem at last,' Josh observed.

'I'm not sure I want to know about it,' Sophie murmured. She gave herself a mental shake and smiled brightly. 'How was your weekend?'

'Fantastic.' Josh stretched his back as he straightened. 'And yours?'

'It was OK. Pretty quiet,' she added nonchalantly.

'I expect you're missing Greg.'

Sophie's hand shook at the unexpected sympathy in Josh's tone, and the instant coffee spilled onto the bench. She grabbed the dishcloth. For a wild moment Sophie considered confiding in Josh Cooper. Instinct persuaded her otherwise. Josh had a close friendship with his professional partner. His own off-duty life-style appeared to be dedicated to squeezing the maximum possible enjoyment out of life—and women. Fun times only. Anything serious had to be fobbed off, usually via the long-suffering co-operation of Toni Marsh. Josh had been horrified by Sophie's lack of experience in relationships and would probably cheer Oliver on in offering to provide a comparison. Perhaps they got on so well because they were two of a kind.

Oliver entered the staffroom just as Sophie finished wiping down the bench and had managed a slightly embarrassed smile in response to Josh's concern. But Josh didn't see the smile. He was looking at his partner.

'Our Sophie's not too happy this morning,' he informed Oliver.

'Really?' Oliver's concern was quite genuine. He hadn't meant to frighten Sophie by kissing her. He could have kicked himself for giving in to that overwhelming compulsion, but he'd done his best to back off and lighten things up. That sniping comment about his marriage had helped quite a lot at the time but it was becoming difficult again. Damned difficult. He couldn't look at her for more than an instant or two, and when they were alone he tried to imagine Greg standing protectively beside her. That wasn't easy as he had no idea what the man looked like. Probably seven feet tall with a red cape and knickers on the outside of his trousers. Surely Sophie wouldn't settle for anyone less compelling?

Sophie could feel the laser-like beam of Oliver's full attention coming at her. She refused to respond and concentrated carefully on spooning coffee into her mug.

'She's missing Greg,' Josh explained kindly.

'Are you, Sophie?' Oliver's quiet words had all the effect of mortar shells. Sophie had to move. She had to try and decrease the sense of awareness his proximity raised in her body. Sophie tried to summon some of the anger left over from the weekend's emotional turmoil before she made eye contact.

'Yes,' she admitted calmly. 'I am missing Greg.' She picked up her mug. 'I'll take this with me,' she announced. 'It's time I started earning my keep.'

It hadn't been a dishonest statement. Sophie left her mug on her desk and headed for the waiting room. She *was* missing Greg. She was missing the comfortable security of their relationship, the knowledge that she had a declared ally, no matter what life might throw at her in the future. A good friend. A *really* good friend. Was she really so sure it wasn't enough of a base for a good marriage?

'Mrs Murdock? Would you like to come through now?'

Ruby Murdock was looking very pleased with herself. 'I've kept up my diary every day and I've taken my puffer every morning. I get Felicity to check up on me when she comes.'

'How often have you needed to use your Ventolin inhaler?'

'Oh, a few times. But things are a lot better.'

'You haven't made a note of when you've needed the Ventolin in your diary.'

'Didn't I? Oh, I'm sorry, dear.' Ruby looked apologetic. 'It must have slipped my mind.'

'You've done very well, keeping up your peak-flow

chart,' Sophie said encouragingly. 'We can work out an asthma action plan for you now and give you some guidelines on what treatment you might need and when. It'll mean you'll be able to manage your own asthma much more effectively.'

Ruby looked doubtful. Then her gaze shifted to Sophie's coffee-mug and she licked her lips. Sophie pushed her mug further away.

'Do you know, I've had four cups of tea already this morning and I'm still thirsty?' Ruby was still watching the mug.

'Really? Do you usually drink so much tea in the mornings?'

'I have lately but I really must stop.' Ruby sighed. 'It's getting annoying, having to get up so many times at night.'

The possibility of diabetes was Sophie's first thought. 'I want to test your blood-sugar level,' she informed her patient as she lifted a blood-glucose testing kit from her cupboard. 'I'll just need to prick your finger.'

Sophie ran through the appropriate history-taking, examination and lab tests she might need to instigate while she waited the sixty seconds for the meter to finish counting.

'Nineteen mmol per litre,' she read out. 'That's rather too high, Mrs Murdock.'

'Is that because of my asthma, dear?'

'No. High blood sugar is usually indicative of diabetes. I'm going to check you out thoroughly and then we'll have a chat about your diet and exercise routines. Come and stand on the scales for me.'

'Oh, dear.' Ruby moved reluctantly towards the

scales. 'I do hope you're not going to tell me I have to eat salad.'

An hour later, Sophie had told Ruby Murdock a great deal about her diet and the need to start some exercise.

'I'm going to write you out what we call a green prescription. You don't take it to the chemist but it's still very important,' she told Ruby firmly. 'It's going to be for a ten-minute walk once a day. Do you think you can manage just ten minutes?'

'I expect so, dear.' Ruby nodded bravely.

'And you might even think about your housework. Vacuuming is very good exercise.' Sophie tried to keep her tone professional. 'Felicity does that for you, doesn't she?'

'Oh, yes. She's doing it right now. I'm going to ring when I'm ready to go home. My wrist is still very weak,' Ruby continued anxiously. 'I couldn't possibly manage the vacuuming.'

Sophie made a note to refer Ruby to a physiotherapist. She wouldn't mention it today. They both had quite enough to think about. Sophie hunted Oliver down between his patients. She was concerned enough about Ruby to put her personal agenda with her supervisor entirely to one side. Oliver responded in kind. He appeared to be listening carefully to Sophie but she couldn't help noticing that he tended to look to one side of her. It gave her the eerie feeling that she had someone standing beside her. She took a quick glance herself. No one else was waiting silently for Oliver's attention.

'I've ordered fasting glucose tests, a lipid profile, serum creatinine, haemoglobin and a urine analysis,' Sophie told him briskly. 'Have I missed anything?'

'What's her blood pressure like?'

'Borderline. One-forty over ninety.'

'Asthma control?'

'Improving.'

'What's her BMI?'

Sophie shook her head. Ruby's body mass index was clinically obese. 'Thirty-one,' she told Oliver. 'Her weight's been going up steadily for years. Should I have started her on active treatment? Like metformin?'

'Not yet. When's she getting the lab tests done?'

'She's going to see if Felicity can take her in tomorrow.' The glance Sophie shared with Oliver acknowledged the increasing pressure on Ruby Murdock's daughter.

'Wait for the results,' Oliver advised. 'I'll go through them with you and I might sit in on the next visit. It's turning into quite a complicated case for you.'

'It's good practice.' Sophie smiled, partly from relief that she could still interact on a professional level with Oliver despite her mixed personal feelings. 'But I've spend far too long with one patient.'

'That's exactly why we don't give you too many,' Oliver reassured her. 'So you can take whatever time you need to be thorough. You've done well, Sophie. Diabetes is an important problem to have picked up on.'

Sophie carried her cold cup of coffee to the staff-room and tipped it out. Janet was sitting on the couch with Toni.

'Hi, Janet. Did you have a good weekend?'

'No. It was an unmitigated disaster. I've just been telling Toni all about it.'

'What happened?' Sophie tried not to sound eager to hear but at least there was someone else who hadn't enjoyed their break from work.

'Dennis,' Janet said gloomily.

'Oh.' Sophie sat down with her fresh coffee. Dennis was a real-estate agent Janet had met several weeks ago when he had marketed a neighbouring property. So far the dates had been very successful. Dennis was wealthy, stylish and very keen on Janet. 'I take it the evening at home with the boys didn't go so well?'

Toni giggled. 'Rory told Dennis that he was a dork.'

'Oh, no!' Sophie bit her lip.

'If the boys hadn't built that possum trap in the back garden it wouldn't have been a problem.'

'Have you got possums?' Sophie queried.

'Not that I know of.' Janet grinned. 'Adam and Rory just wanted to make a trap. They dug this big hole and covered it with twigs and leaves. Then it started raining and they came inside and forgot about it.'

'They didn't tell Janet they had built it near the woodshed,' Toni added.

'And Dennis very helpfully offered to get some wood in for the fire while I was getting dinner ready,' Janet continued. 'He stepped in the possum trap and fell face down into the muddiest part of the garden. Rory and Adam were watching from the upstairs window. Dennis was naturally furious at their amusement, and when I hauled them down to apologise Rory said it wasn't their fault that I was going out with a dork.'

Sophie laughed. Even Janet was sounding amused.

'He said he was going home to change his suit. Only he never came back.'

'Not father material, then,' Sophie noted.

'Apparently not.' Janet looked resigned. 'I don't know why I keep trying.'

'Because the boys need a father,' Toni reminded her. 'You've been saying so for years.'

'Yes—but I don't think I need a man,' Janet groaned. 'The good ones are too hard to find.'

'You're telling me.' Toni smiled at Sophie. 'At least one of us has got lucky.'

'Why don't you get the boys into a club of some sort?' Sophie suggested quickly, trying to deflect the attention from herself. 'Something with a male role model. Like rugby or Scouts.'

'They're too young for Scouts,' Janet responded. 'They'd like to go to Cubs but the uniforms are awfully expensive. A lot of their friends go.'

'Sounds ideal,' Sophie encouraged. 'What's the cubmaster like?'

Toni grinned. 'Is he single?'

'I believe so.' Janet rolled her eyes. 'I've also heard that he likes knitting.'

Toni laughed, getting to her feet. 'Come on. Time to get back to the grind. Forget the cubmaster. Nobody's that desperate. Even me!'

The last of Ruby Murdock's results came back on Thursday. The last few days had seen a kind of unspoken truce between Sophie and Oliver. They had both withdrawn to a space that precluded any interaction of a personal nature. Oliver hadn't flirted—not once—and Sophie had relaxed her guard enough to smile a little more often.

'You've got diabetes, Mrs Murdock,' Sophie confirmed, having explained the results. 'You've also got a rather high cholesterol level.'

'Oh.' Ruby looked apprehensive but then smiled at Sophie. 'I expect you'll want to give me some pills, then, dear.'

'Not immediately.' Sophie glanced at Oliver who nodded encouragement. 'It's quite possible that these issues can be successfully treated with some lifestyle changes.' Her gaze included Felicity King who was sitting beside her mother. 'That's why I thought it would be a good idea if Felicity came in with you today. We want to get your cholesterol level down and help you lose some weight. That means you need to make changes to your diet and your level of activity.'

'I've been going for walks,' Ruby protested. 'Every day since I saw you on Monday. Today will be the third time.'

'That's great, Ruby,' Oliver nodded. 'It's a very good start. Keep it up.'

Ruby beamed. 'It was Dr Bennett's green prescription. I feel I have to do it.'

'I have the list we made on Monday, Mrs Murdock.' Sophie caught Felicity's eye. 'All those wonderful dinners Felicity makes for you. Did you read that pamphlet I gave you on high-fat foods?'

'I did,' Felicity said. 'And I've told Mum I'm not doing any more roasts for her. Or pies.'

Ruby gave her daughter a wounded look. Felicity sighed heavily.

'There are some very good low-fat meals you can buy in the supermarket,' Sophie suggested. 'I know they're a little expensive but you just need to heat them up in the microwave. I use them myself quite often. It's very easy and you don't need to change everything at once. We'll tackle one step at a time.'

'Felicity likes cooking for me,' Ruby stated. 'Don't you, dear?'

'Well, actually, Mum…' Felicity cast an appealing glance at Sophie. Oliver cleared his throat and stood up.

'I'll leave you to it, Dr Bennett. I'm sure you'll all sort out a great plan.'

Sophie made sure she caught Oliver before her next patient.

'How could you?' she groaned. 'I ended up mediating emotional warfare between mother and daughter.'

'Good practice,' Oliver grinned, and suddenly the tension of the last week evaporated. The warmth was there again. The barrier was down. Oliver's expression became more serious. 'How did it go?'

'I think we made some progress,' Sophie said hopefully. 'Ruby's got the idea that she might be asking a bit much of Felicity. She's going to get her exercise by walking to the supermarket every other day. It's only ten minutes away and that'll save Felicity having to take her shopping once a week. She's also going to try cooking for herself once or twice a week. She didn't look very happy about it all, though.'

'Did Felicity look any happier?'

'No.' Sophie sighed worriedly. 'I think her mother's very good at making her feel guilty. It's going to be an effort for both of them to make changes.'

'When are you seeing Ruby again?'

'Next week. She'll need lots of encouragement to

keep going. Janet's going to monitor her weight and throw in a few pep talks.'

'Good. It can be a big effort to make changes.' Oliver's gaze dropped suddenly to Sophie's left hand and she felt a familiar prickle. Ruby Murdock wasn't the only one capable of stirring up guilt feelings.

'How's the finger?'

'Fine.' Sophie waggled the digit in question. 'I was going to take the steri-strips off today.'

'Great. I'll do it for you.'

'There's no need.' Even the thought of Oliver's hands touching her own deliberately caused a minor sensation of panic, panic that could actually be stirrings of the desire Sophie had thought she had successfully suppressed.

'I'd like to have a look. After all, I did treat it. Come on, to the treatment room.' Oliver was holding the door open. 'I've only got the repeat prescriptions to do for the next half-hour and they won't mind waiting.'

'I've got some reading I really need to do on Type Two diabetes,' Sophie protested. 'I was just going to make a start.'

'That can wait, too,' Oliver declared. 'You've been buried with your books or dashing off to tutorials or workshops all week. Anyone would think you were suddenly trying to avoid us all.'

Sophie had no answer to that. She doubted whether any protest would sound convincing enough. It was, after all, quite true.

'Now, let's have a look.' Oliver cradled Sophie's hand in his as he unwound the gauze bandage. He inspected the cut on her finger with close attention. 'Looks lovely,' he pronounced. His grip on her hand tightened as he glanced up. 'Just like the rest of you,' he added softly.

Sophie was still speechless. So it had just been an interlude, a few days' respite in the campaign Oliver had launched to draw her into his bed. This was the opportunity she had waited for all week. The chance to put Oliver Spencer in his place. To let him know precisely what she thought of the male gender's attitude to sex in general and Oliver Spencer's attitude in particular. She knew her lips had parted but the right words weren't available.

She could feel the distance between herself and Oliver closing. Slowly. Too slowly. Sophie knew perfectly well that Oliver Spencer was about to kiss her. She also knew that she *wanted* Oliver Spencer to kiss her. Wanted it desperately.

'Ooh, sorry! Am I interrupting something?' Janet's wildly curly head was just visible past Oliver's shoulder. He adjusted the distance between himself and Sophie smoothly, transferring his eye contact to his practice nurse.

'Not at all, Jan. I'm just going to take these steristrips off Sophie's finger. You couldn't find a bit of plaster or something, could you? It'll still need to be kept covered.'

'I've got just the thing.' Janet produced a sticking plaster adorned with Disney characters. She peered at Sophie's finger. 'I didn't realise you had to use yourself as a guinea pig in those minor surgery workshops.'

'You don't.' Sophie tried to smile but her lips trembled. 'Some of us are just a little over-enthusiastic.'

Oliver caught her eye. The movement of his eyebrows and mouth suggested that she might be referring to what Janet's entrance had circumvented. 'Enthusiasm can be a very good attribute,' he said quietly. 'I'm all in favour of it myself.'

'That's fine,' Sophie agreed, meeting his gaze squarely. 'Provided someone doesn't end up getting hurt.'

Oliver stuck the plaster down gently. 'There. I'm afraid you still won't fit your ring on.'

'Just as well you weren't wearing it when you cut your finger,' Janet observed. 'It would have been painful getting it off.'

'Maybe it was painful anyway,' Oliver muttered. Sophie gave him a sharp glance which caused his lips to curve unrepentantly. 'I mean, after five years it could have been almost ingrown.'

'You're as bad as Josh,' Janet admonished. 'You both seem to be allergic to anything long term in the way of relationships. What's so wrong with a bit of commitment?'

'Oh, nothing at all.' Oliver glanced back over his shoulder as he dropped the rubbish he had collected into the bin. 'As long as it's going somewhere. Do you play chess, Jan?'

'No.' Janet winked at Sophie. 'But I'm considering taking up knitting.'

'Try chess,' Oliver advised as he headed for the door. 'You'll find out that both winning and losing can be exciting. But there's nothing worse than a stalemate.'

'I'd settle for a mate.' Janet grinned cheekily after Oliver had gone. 'Stale or otherwise.'

'No, you wouldn't,' Sophie contradicted firmly. 'That's why you're still single: You're waiting for exactly the right person. Like me.'

Janet glanced at Sophie with a curious expression. 'But you never had to wait. You've got Greg.'

'Mmm.' Sophie fought off a wave of despair. 'I guess I'm not in any position to hand out advice. But don't listen to Oliver either. It's not about winning and losing. If a relationship is going to mean anything, I think it has to be more than just a game.'

Oliver thought it was a game. He didn't even care if he won or lost. He just wanted to play.

And he wanted to play with Sophie.

CHAPTER FIVE

Sophie wasn't going to play with Oliver Spencer.

She wasn't going to play with any man. Subterfuge went against all her basic principles and it was no wonder she felt so disturbed. Being less than honest was lowering herself to Oliver's level. A flirtatious comment here, a double meaning or lie by omission there. Deception, for whatever reason, was unacceptable and even self-protection wasn't a good excuse. Sophie Bennett knew what she wanted out of life and out of a relationship. Nobody, and particularly Oliver Spencer, was going to manipulate her into settling for anything less.

When you stopped looking for them, opportunities presented themselves quite easily. Sophie hadn't anticipated the direction the conversation would take when Janet pointed out a page in the magazine she was browsing through at lunchtime.

'Look at that!' she exclaimed. 'Milford Sound. Isn't that the most beautiful place you could ever imagine?'

'You have to tramp for days to get there,' Toni told her. 'Heavy backpacks, sore feet. You'd be too exhausted to appreciate the view once you got there.'

Sophie laughed. 'It's not that bad. I love tramping.'

'Do you?' Josh looked surprised. 'I hadn't picked you for a hardy outdoors type.'

'I'll bet Graham loves tramping, too,' Oliver observed drily. 'I can just imagine him throwing up a tent single-handed.' He sipped his coffee thoughtfully. 'And making a fire with just a few twigs to rub together.'

'His name's Greg,' Sophie corrected wearily. 'He's not a Scout.' She threw Oliver a long-suffering glance. 'And he did love tramping. We just haven't had time for anything like that for years.' Sophie fiddled with the sticking plaster on her finger. 'In fact, we haven't really had much time together for years.'

'That sounds like a bit of a problem,' Toni sympathised.

'Oh, I don't know.' Josh was grinning broadly. 'Sounds like a great way to keep a relationship going. Don't see each other.'

Toni ignored Josh. 'You'll have more time once you get married,' she reassured Sophie. 'Maybe you can go tramping on your honeymoon.'

'There isn't going to be a honeymoon,' Sophie heard herself announce quietly.

'Why—is Greg too busy?' It was Oliver's turn to sound sympathetic. 'We can always give you some time off here. No problem.'

Sophie kept her gaze on the table. 'It's not just that,' she said determinedly. 'There are other things.'

There was a short silence around the table.

'Have you had a row with Greg?' Janet asked tentatively.

'Not exactly.' Sophie bit her lip.

'You haven't broken your engagement, have you?' Toni sounded horrified. 'But you've been together for years! You love each other.'

'There are different kinds of love,' Sophie said cautiously. 'Different levels. I don't think what Greg and I have is strong enough for marriage.'

'Nonsense.' Oliver was looking worried. Did he think Sophie might blame him publicly for changing her mind? 'You're just getting cold feet now that you've finally taken the plunge and set a date.'

'We haven't set a date,' Sophie said miserably. 'I just made that up.'

The silence around the table was longer this time as her colleagues digested Sophie's confession. She braved a quick look around the group. Janet and Josh both looked curious. Toni looked dismayed. Oliver looked unexpectedly disappointed.

'I'm sure you had a good reason,' he said coolly. 'I mean, you wouldn't have invented a date if it wasn't something you really wanted.'

'If it was something we really wanted it would have happened years ago,' Sophie said a little desperately. 'Maybe Josh was right. I haven't had enough experience when it comes to relationships.'

'I'm never right when it comes to relationships,' Josh said lightly. 'Don't listen to me, Sophie.'

'No, don't,' Toni agreed hastily. 'Just look at Josh's track record.'

'You can't give up that easily,' Janet added. 'Not after you've been together so long.'

Oliver was nodding seriously. 'Commitment is like honesty, Sophie. It's not something to give or take lightly.'

'I know.' Sophie stared at Oliver. What was he trying to do now? Persuade her to go back to Greg? Had she been correct in thinking that it had only been her unavailability that had made her attractive?

'Try and make it up with him,' Toni urged her. 'I'm sure it's not too late.'

Oliver looked away from Sophie. He pushed himself to his feet with a heavy sigh.

'Toni's quite right,' he told Sophie. 'It's never too late. Not when it's something you really want.' He glanced at his watch. 'Ross Selkirk is coming in for his mole removal in ten minutes. Do you still want to have a go at some minor surgery?'

'Oh, yes!' Sophie got to her feet hurriedly. 'I'd love to, if it's still all right with you. You'll have to supervise me, though. I haven't done one before.'

Oliver was waiting by the door for Sophie to catch up. 'Of course I'll supervise you.' He seemed to collect his thoughts and then he smiled cheerfully. 'It's precisely what I'm supposed to be doing with you, after all.'

So that's that, Sophie decided, trailing after Oliver to the treatment room. Even the thought of her being available had made Oliver retreat to his professional position. More than that, he'd deliberately given her a push back in Greg's direction. She had tampered with the rules of the game and Oliver didn't want to play any more. Well, fine. If he could put aside physical attraction and go back to how they had been when she'd first arrived at St David's, then so could she.

With something as interesting as minor surgery to concentrate on, it was actually remarkably easy. She was almost unaware of the pressure of Oliver's leg as he stood close beside her a short time later, peering over her shoulder.

'That's great. You've got a good elliptical incision there. Now catch the edge of the bit you're removing with the tweezers and gently stroke the scalpel down the sides. Try and leave a good margin.'

Sophie nodded, her tongue caught between her top

teeth and bottom lip as she kept her attention focused. Their patient, Ross Selkirk, was the courier who usually attended to St. David's many deliveries and pickups. He hadn't minded a bit when Oliver had suggested that Sophie had a go at her first mole removal. She was determined not to let either of them down. She knew she was slow but it had to be perfect. Sophie swapped the scalpel for the scissors to snip one particularly tough adhesion.

'There,' she said eventually. She turned to drop the patch of skin and tissue into the specimen jar half full of formalin. At the same time Oliver moved to swab the incision site with a gauze pad. Their arms brushed but neither seemed to notice.

'What suture are you going to use, Sophie?'

'Five-O?'

'Good.' Oliver nodded his approval as he opened the sterile pack for her.

The wound gaped at Sophie like a small, smiling mouth. 'It's not bleeding much at all now,' she observed happily.

'That's the beauty of having the adrenaline in the lignocaine. You can only use plain lignocaine on any digits, though. Bit more bleeding to cope with then.'

Sophie had the curved needle attached to the length of suture thread grasped firmly in the needle holder in her right hand. She held her tweezers ready in her left hand. She inserted the needle through one side of the wound and then the other. She could feel the movement of Oliver's head as he nodded approval again, his head almost touching her shoulder.

'Excellent. How do you judge the width of each bite?'

'Roughly one to two times the thickness of the

skin,' Sophie responded promptly. She pulled the length of suture until only a couple of inches remained, then she wound the thread twice around the needle holder and grasped the short end to slip the loops over it. Sophie smiled with satisfaction as she pulled it tight and the edges of the skin came together neatly. She knotted the stitch and held the ends up. Oliver snipped them off.

The voice of their patient was muffled by the pillow his head was buried in. 'How many stitches are you going to need, do you think?'

'Only three, Ross,' Sophie told him. 'Are you OK? I know I'm being a bit slower than Dr Spencer would have been.'

'I'm fine,' Ross said. 'Take as long as you like. This is a sight more relaxing than fighting traffic to try and get places on time.'

Sophie put her second suture at the other end of the wound. 'Work from the outside in,' she muttered to Oliver. 'One side, then the other. Leave the centre till last.' This time she did the loops around the needle holder more confidently. By the third suture the manoeuvre was almost a flourish.

'Cut, thanks,' she ordered Oliver with a grin.

Sophie cleaned up the neat wound with a swab and some Betadine, then covered it with a dressing. 'The stitches can come out in a week to ten days, Ross,' she said. 'We'll phone you as soon as we get the lab results. It doesn't look nasty but it pays to be careful, especially when it's been itchy like that.'

'Thanks, Doc.' Ross sat up and reached for his red and white shirt.

'You're welcome.' Sophie smiled broadly. 'I really enjoyed that.'

'I'll ask for you first next time, then.'

Oliver looked resigned. 'I see I'm going to have some competition for any minor surgery going around here. It's always been my specialty.'

'I'm sure you don't mind having Dr Bennett around.' Ross's gaze was openly admiring as Sophie passed him his red and white anorak. 'I know I wouldn't.'

Oliver's smile was automatic. 'We all love having Sophie around,' he said casually. 'Though unfortunately it's only temporary. She has someone waiting for her in Auckland.'

'Oh.' Ross nodded as though it was only to be expected. 'Lucky man.'

'Indeed,' Oliver agreed. Sophie waited in some trepidation for Oliver's next comment as Ross left the room, but Oliver merely raised his eyebrows. 'What have you got lined up for the rest of the afternoon, Sophie?'

'A study period next but I've got Pagan Ellis coming in later.' Sophie paused in the clean-up of the sterile tray, having dropped the metal instruments back into the kidney dish for Janet to re-sterilise. 'Would you sit in on that consult with me? I'm really not happy, trying to deal with something this way out.'

'Just lay the risks on the line for her,' Oliver advised. 'Be specific. Ask her if she really wants to end up with major difficulties and a dead baby miles from anywhere. You'll see, she'll book in at Women's with an obstetrical consultant on standby in no time flat.'

'Hmm.' Sophie was unconvinced. 'So I can call you if I'm not getting anywhere, then?'

'Of course.' Oliver's gaze was sincere. 'I'm here

for you, anytime you need me, Sophie. You know that.'

Sophie dropped the used gloves and dressings into the rubbish bag and slotted the scalpel into the sealed sharps container. She took another quick glance at Oliver. No. There wasn't even a hint of any sexual undertone to his comment. He was offering professional support. Just as he had when she had first arrived. He looked as though he had never even considered offering anything else.

'Thanks,' Sophie murmured. 'I'm sure I can cope.'

Periods of time set aside for Sophie to study were a regular part of her timetable at St David's, but the subject she found herself pondering that afternoon had little to do with the practice of medicine.

She had tried to put things right but, instead of helping, it seemed to have made things worse. What had she expected? She'd known Oliver's interest might not last, but to have it evaporate before he'd even tried to follow it through was confusing. Not to mention humiliating. If he hadn't found something desirable in that first kiss why had he almost tried again this morning?

God! Just the thought of that second attempt was enough to make Sophie's pulse thump painfully. She would have kissed him back, too. And more. Was she so naïve and inexperienced that she couldn't recognise the power of physical attraction? Maybe Greg had been right. The flames of a passionate sexual attraction never lasted and easily blinded someone to a lover's real personality. Love wasn't blind but lust certainly was. What Sophie Bennett was feeling for Oliver Spencer had to be lust. Why else would she have failed to heed the warning signs of sheer arrogance, amply demonstrated again today by his casual implication of attraction and his equally casual withdrawal? Why else would she be feeling such an acute physical frustration right now?

Oliver could switch it off—as easily as if it was a card to be discarded in the hand he was playing. It meant nothing. He had said it himself. Oliver wasn't planning to ride off into a blissful sunset with her. He was merely offering a comparison. A sort of free sample of what might still be available out there. Perhaps it was normal behaviour in the adult world. Sophie had seen and read enough to know about casual attitudes to sexual relationships. She wasn't *that* naïve.

Sophie had never learned the rules of the game Oliver was playing because she had never been tempted to join in. Until now. And she still wasn't going to play, however powerful the physical incentive. She was quite experienced enough to know that if she played with fire she was very likely to get burnt.

Oliver Spencer didn't want her. Not on any meaningful level. He thought she should make things up with Greg and reinstate her engagement. Maybe he was right. It would be far safer to abandon the fire the likes of Oliver Spencer represented and stay with the warm glow she had always previously been satisfied with. Safer and much easier. Sophie nodded slowly to herself. She would ring Greg. If he agreed, she would resign her registrar post and move back to Auckland. Take a job in the hospital or another general practice. She would put her life back on the rails. If she cut Oliver Spencer out of her existence now, any wound would soon heal. The danger lay in allowing the vulnerability to deepen, and Sophie was not about to become an emotional victim.

The phone in Sophie's office was internal so it couldn't be used for a toll call. The reception area was fortunately deserted. Toni was making her usual daily visit to the bank and post office just down the road. Janet was looking after the desk and the phones but was at present ushering a Mrs Kincaid into the treatment room for a flu shot.

'You realise you'll need to wait for twenty minutes after the vaccination, Mrs Kincaid?' Janet queried. 'That's just so we can be sure you're not going to have any kind of adverse reaction.'

'That's fine, Nurse. I've got nothing very important to do this afternoon.'

Sophie waited until the door of the treatment room swung closed. She picked up one of the phones on Toni's desk and dialled quickly.

'Could you page Dr Greg Hayes for me, please?' Sophie asked the operator. 'His beep number is 374.'

'Sophie!' Greg sounded astonished. 'Is something wrong?'

'No. I just wanted to talk to you.' Sophie found herself smiling at Greg's familiar voice. 'I…I've been thinking about you.'

'You're lucky you caught me. I'm just on my way to an ICU staff conference. The pace is frantic up here at the moment. We've got a patient overflow that's hitting crisis level.'

'Sorry. I know you're busy. I've tried ringing you at home a few times. You never seem to be there.'

'No.' Greg sounded embarrassed. 'I'm out a fair bit.' There was a short, awkward pause. 'Did you get the flowers?'

'Yes, thank you. It was sweet of you. That was really why I was ringing. I wanted to say I thought you might be…' Sophie searched for some way to tell Greg she had changed her mind, but the words didn't want to come out. Did she really believe that Greg had been right? Did she really want to put things back the way they had been?

'Missing you?' Greg broke the pause. 'Of course I am. But you were right, you know, Soph. When I really thought about it I realised exactly what our relationship had been missing, and…'

'And?' Sophie prompted. Suddenly she wished she hadn't made this call.

'And…ah…I'm not sure how to say this.' Greg sounded as though he also wished Sophie hadn't made the call.

'You've found someone else?' Sophie suggested. She tried to laugh. 'That was quick, Greg.'

Greg cleared his throat loudly. 'We've been working together for ages. I guess I'd been ignoring the spark between us but you made me take another look.'

Sophie couldn't help a faintly derisive snort. So she had been responsible?

'It would never have come to anything, Soph, if you hadn't decided… I mean, I don't want you to think I was cheating on you or anything.'

'No. That's OK, Greg. I understand.' Sophie was aware of Janet returning to the office area behind her. She could hear the files in one of the in-baskets being shuffled. She held the phone more tightly against her ear and lowered her voice.

'We'll always be friends,' Greg said gently. 'Very special friends. I do love you, Soph. You know that, don't you?'

'Yes, I know.' Sophie pressed her lips together to

hold back the tears. She took a deep breath. 'I feel the same way, Greg. I love you, too.'

She put the phone down slowly. That was that, then. She'd burnt her bridges or perhaps her bolt hole. Strangely, the effect was one of relief. Going backwards would have been a huge mistake. Greg might make a good friend but, as far as a partner in a marriage went, he had just revealed a rather telling inadequacy. Greg was no different to any other man when it came to the crunch. Five minutes without her and he'd already found a replacement. Sophie knew she shouldn't blame Greg. Perhaps it was just her pride that was wounded.

Sophie shook her head, still staring at the phone. Fancy being rejected twice on the same day. Oliver wanted her to go back to Greg. And Greg didn't want her back. Was she missing something important here? Still grappling with the new and rather disturbing notion, Sophie turned to find herself under intense scrutiny. Not, as she had expected, from Janet Muir, but from Oliver Spencer.

When had he come in? He was holding a patient file. Dimly, Sophie remembered hearing the files being sorted. Just before Greg had told her he loved her. Before she had repeated the same vow. She could see the echoes of it in Oliver's dark eyes. Sophie straightened her spine. What did she care what Oliver thought? Right now, she'd had quite enough of dealing with men. Sophie turned away and leaned over the counter.

'Pagan? Would you like to come through now?'

If Pagan Ellis's pregnancy was starting to show it was well disguised by the flowing, long dress in shades of orange and crimson. Her thick, dark hair was piled on top of her head today, with long, curling wisps catching on the large, hooped earrings.

'I've decided,' Pagan told Sophie breathlessly. 'On the beach.'

'Have you?' Sophie tried to sound interested. 'Can you take your shawl off for a minute so I can take your blood pressure?'

The tangle of bracelets and bangles made their familiar musical accompaniment to Pagan's movements. She took no notice of Sophie winding the cuff around her upper arm.

'Dolphin Point,' she said dreamily. 'Isn't that perfect?'

'I have no idea where it is,' Sophie confessed. She put her stethoscope into position and began to deflate the cuff slowly.

'It's out on the Banks Peninsula,' Pagan informed her. 'Sort of across the harbour from Akaroa.'

Sophie silently finished her measurement. She removed the cuff, folded her stethoscope and sat down at her desk to record the result, still silently. She put the pen down carefully and looked directly at Pagan.

'That would be at least two hours' drive from Christchurch,' she said flatly.

'Plus the boat ride.' Pagan grinned. 'There's four-wheel-drive access to the beach but it's a bit of a long haul and I've only got my bike. I don't drive.'

'Neither do I,' Sophie said firmly. 'At least, not that far and especially not that far to try and deliver a baby.'

Pagan Ellis was unperturbed. 'My midwife, Wendy, has got a four-wheel-drive. She's quite happy to give you a ride. She's really keen. I think she wants

to end up on the six o'clock news for the most unusual birth story.'

'The birth might very well end up on the six
o'clock news,' Sophie told Pagan seriously. 'It might
well be a disaster story involving the death of a
mother and/or her baby due to unforeseen complications. I imagine the hunt for whoever was responsible
for medical care and the criticism for allowing it to
happen would be an absolute feast for the media.'

'Oh, nothing's going to go wrong,' Pagan said se-
renely. 'I've had a tarot reading and my clairvoyant
is quite happy. I've been going to her for years. It's
really hard to get an appointment. She's booked up
for months in advance. People fly in from all over the
country to see her. She knows what she's talking
about.'

'I'm sure she does.' Sophie wondered, briefly,
whether the clairvoyant's bank balance was healthier
than her own. 'But I know what I'm talking about,
too, Pagan, and I'm not happy at all. I'm a GP registrar. I haven't had a lot of experience with even
normal deliveries, but I do know some of the complications that would be impossible to deal with outside a hospital setting.'

Sophie proceeded to list the complications. Even
graphic scenarios of severe haemorrhage, hypovo-
laemic shock and death didn't appear to register with
her patient. Pagan waited until she had finished and
then smiled.

'I took that prescription you gave me for the multi-
vitamin tablets when I went to see Iris. She's my
clairvoyant, you know.'

'Very appropriate name,' Sophie murmured.

'Anyway, she knew just by holding it that you were

the right person. I have every faith in you, Sophie.'
She leaned forward eagerly. 'I want you to share this
experience with me. I think you'll find it life-
changing.'

'That's what bothers me.' Sophie was feeling worn
down by Pagan's unshakeable convictions. She decided she would have to back off for the moment.
'Did you think about the blood tests and ultrasound
scan I suggested?'

'No.' Pagan shook her head and a few more ten-
drils of hair floated loose. 'I mean, yes, I did think
about it and, no, I don't want them.'

Sophie saw a glimmer of hope. 'These tests are
really the only way of getting any sort of reassurance
that the birth will be uncomplicated. I would feel a
lot happier about this if I had some evidence that the
pregnancy is normal.'

'Would you?' Pagan looked surprised.

'Ultrasound is the way dolphins communicate, you
know, Pagan.' Sophie felt suddenly inspired. 'Bounc-
ing sound waves off things to get a picture. It's the
same idea with a scan of the baby. Quite an Aquarius
thing, I would have thought.'

Pagan's eyes shone. 'You're quite right, Sophie.
Book me in, then.' She jumped to her feet.

Sophie held the door open with some relief and
took her down to see Toni.

'Pagan wants a scan booked at Women's, please,
Toni. In a fortnight. She'll be about fifteen weeks by
then.'

Pagan leaned over the counter and nodded wisely
at Toni. 'I *knew* Sophie was the right person. I'm
never wrong about auras.'

* * *

'So! You've persuaded Pagan Ellis to have a scan.' Oliver's head appeared around Sophie's door later that afternoon. 'That was well done.'

'It wasn't all that difficult,' Sophie said modestly. 'I still need to talk her into having the routine blood tests and maybe even amniocentesis, but I am rather pleased, I must say. It's a bit of a relief, really.'

'I'm sure it is.' Oliver stepped inside the room and closed the door behind him. 'You've had quite a productive afternoon. You've sorted out a difficult patient and your relationship.'

'Sorry?' Sophie's eyes widened.

'I wasn't eavesdropping intentionally.' Oliver's smile was a little forced. 'But it sounded like you patched things up with Greg quite nicely.'

Sophie shrugged. 'There wasn't anything to patch up,' she said levelly. 'Not any more.'

Oliver frowned. 'Didn't I hear you tell the man you loved him?'

'As a friend, yes,' Sophie agreed. 'That's all.'

'Did Greg know that?' Oliver's question was surprisingly sharp. 'How did he feel about that?'

Sophie stared at Oliver accusingly. 'I don't remember you being very concerned about Greg's feelings when you offered yourself as a comparison.'

'Perhaps you're wrong.' Oliver folded his arms and leaned back against the door. 'Every man deserves to be sure that his future wife is being honest with him. Did you tell him about the wedding date you had planned?'

Sophie said nothing.

'Have you told him that you're not wearing your engagement ring any more? That even the dateless wedding is off?'

Sophie still remained silent.

'Who are you really lying to, Sophie?' Oliver inquired softly. 'Greg—or me? Or are you just trying to keep your options open?'

'Why would I do that?' Sophie felt genuinely bemused by the accusation. What on earth had she done to provoke this attack from Oliver?

'To check out whether there's something better on offer. Like most women do.'

'It that what you think I'm doing?' Sophie felt all the anger Oliver had generated the first time he'd kissed her return in full force. 'You've got a real nerve, Oliver Spencer. I didn't ask you to flirt with me. I certainly didn't ask you to kiss me.'

'You didn't exactly fight me off either,' Oliver said smugly. 'Or tell me to get lost.'

Oliver's tone was infuriating. It was her fault that Oliver had made advances because she hadn't said anything to put him off. It was her fault that Greg had found another woman because Sophie *had* said something to make him look. Couldn't men take responsibility for their own actions? In love with this man? Huh! She didn't even *like* him!

'Shall I tell you now, then?' Sophie asked coldly. 'Read my lips, Oliver Spencer. I am not interested in you as anything other than my supervisor in general practice training.' Her mouth twisted sardonically. 'In fact, given your low opinion of women, I'm surprised you bother with us at all.'

'I don't usually,' Oliver said slowly. 'My marriage was enough to put me off. I thought maybe you were different.'

Sophie was stung, as much by Oliver's words as the look of disappointment he was wearing. So, she hadn't come up to scratch. Sophie gave in to the urge to defend herself. 'No. Women are all the same, Oliver. The problem is that we want something that men like you aren't capable of providing.'

'Oh?' Oliver expression became guarded. 'And what might that be?'

'Commitment,' Sophie snapped. 'Something that means a lot more than sex.'

'Is that all you think I'm interested in?' Oliver had the nerve to look surprised.

'Of course it is.' Sophie glared at him. 'You're a man, aren't you?'

'So what was the problem with Gary, then?' Oliver demanded. 'Wasn't a five-year engagement enough of a commitment?'

Sophie was furious. 'That's none of your business. At least Greg has never suggested I'm only stringing him along so I can see what else is on offer. He'd never be so insulting.'

'Perhaps you'd better marry the man, then,' Oliver suggested. His tone became sarcastic. 'Before some other woman snaps up such a prize.'

'Perhaps I had,' Sophie snapped. Oliver Spencer's charm was definitely superficial. The man was arrogant, cynical and downright offensive. If she'd only known his real opinion of women she could have dealt with him a lot sooner than this. 'And perhaps you'd better find a woman who's as shallow-minded as you are and put the rest of us out of our misery.'

Oliver blinked in surprise. He was silent for a moment, searching Sophie's face as she glared angrily at him. His own expression seemed to soften. His lips twitched as though he was trying not to smile. 'Did you have someone in mind?'

Sophie snorted incredulously. If Oliver thought he could appease her by switching on the charm, he was very much mistaken. She'd had enough exposure to gain immunity. 'I'm sure Josh could help you out,' she said dismissively. 'I'm beginning to think you're two of a kind.'

'Typical men,' Oliver nodded. 'Only interested in sex.'

'Exactly.' Sophie looked at Oliver resentfully. Did he find something amusing about all this? 'In fact, hasn't he already found you someone?'

'Oh? Who?'

'Christine.' Sophie announced airily.

'Christine?' Oliver rolled the name around his tongue. He looked blankly at Sophie.

'Christine Prescott. The drug rep,' Sophie explained kindly.

'Ah! Christine of the morning teas, mouse pads and miniskirts.' Oliver pronounced the last observation with relish.

Sophie spoke through gritted teeth. 'That's the one.'

Oliver was staring at Sophie again. His expression was anything but blank. 'Is that what you think I should do, Sophie?'

'It's entirely up to you, Oliver.' Sophie kept her gaze carefully neutral. 'She could well be more receptive to your particular brand of charm than someone like me.'

'Do you think so?' Oliver looked thoughtful. 'You might have something there, I suppose. It's not a bad idea.' Oliver nodded as he reached for the doorhandle. 'Not a bad idea at all, really.'

It was a terrible idea.

Oliver could think of nothing he fancied less than asking Christine Prescott out. Except maybe losing Sophie Bennett for good. She had really got under his skin with her inclusion of him amongst a generalisation of men lacking finesse or the ability to commit themselves. Coming on top of the wave of despair he had experienced, overhearing her telling the wonderful Greg that she loved him, it should have been enough to put off any man in his right mind.

Oliver, however, wasn't in his right mind. He hadn't been since the first moment he had set eyes on Sophie Bennett. About the same moment he had spotted that damned engagement ring twinkling on her finger. OK, so he had teased her a bit, letting her know how much he enjoyed her company, but his antennae had been well tuned to pick up any indication that the attention had been unwelcome.

Maybe he had only been interested in sex initially. It was hard to ignore the blazing desire she aroused in him. But the attraction had gone way beyond that by the time he'd really got to know Sophie. When he'd set out to analyse why he'd felt so jealous of Greg that weekend he had been with Sophie, it hadn't been because the man had had a claim on Sophie's physical attractions. It had been because he had a claim on the rest of her life. It had been the thought of her with someone else for ever that had made Oliver realise just how much he cared. The realisation had been unsettling enough to even make him revise his long-held aversion to the state of matrimony. Maybe, if you chose the right person, it *could* actually work. It could be exactly what Oliver wanted, and needed, to achieve real fulfilment in his life.

When he thought about it all, which happened with

disconcerting regularity, Oliver actually had more to be annoyed about than Sophie. He *had* been encouraged, however unintentional the encouragement had been on Sophie's part. And she *had* lied to him about her wedding date. If she had any inkling at all about how destructive his marriage had been she would know that the fact that Oliver had been prepared to overlook her dishonest behaviour represented a depth of commitment he wouldn't have believed he could still summon.

Maybe he was prepared to forgive the lie because it had been so obvious. Sophie Bennett couldn't lie to save herself. That tell-tale flush on her pale skin. The blaze of guilt in those wide, blue eyes. If anything, Sophie's attempt to deceive him had simply underlined her basic integrity. She hadn't even been able to keep it up. He'd played it cool when she'd confessed. He'd even suggested she had another go at her relationship with Superguy—just to let her know that it wasn't his intention to break up her engagement if that was what she really wanted. He hadn't expected her to rush off and coo over the phone to him, however.

That had been a bit of a shock. So had being told she wasn't interested in him. Was she telling the truth? She'd certainly meant it at the time but, then, why had she radiated pure ice when he'd gone along with her suggestion that he date a bimbo like Christine Prescott? Why should she care? Perhaps she *did* care. Oliver finally relaxed just a little. He'd gone about this all the wrong way. Now what he needed was just a little patience. Women needed time. They liked to mull over alternatives, to think about potential repercussions and worry about them a bit. Maybe what Sophie Bennett needed was a real alternative to mull over. One that might—hopefully—be a little bit of a worry. Or an eye-opener. Like he had been subjected to during that weekend she'd been away.

It sounded like a plan. Oliver wasn't going to give up yet. No way. He smiled to himself. Quite a cheerful smile.

Almost jaunty.

CHAPTER SIX

OLIVER SPENCER had been unusually jaunty all week.

He was smiling a lot. Not that he wasn't normally equable and pleasant but there was a new edge to it that everybody noticed.

'It can't be the weather, that's for sure,' Janet commented. Winter was setting in early with a series of southerlies that boded well for an excellent ski season on nearby Mt Hutt.

The fan heater was running full blast in the waiting room. Several miserable-looking people, who clearly hadn't had their flu shots early enough this season, sat hunched, as far away from each other as possible. A toddler had pulled the old telephone from the toy basket and was shouting enthusiastically enough to make the flu sufferers wince.

'*Ding! Ding! Ding! Ding!* 'Lo! Who's dare?'

'It's Wednesday,' Toni said, casting a slightly weary glance at the toddler. 'Hump day.'

'Hump day?' Sophie queried.

'The hump of the week,' Toni smiled. 'It's all downhill after Wednesday. Have you got a tutorial this afternoon?'

'Yes. Otitis media. Examination of ear canals and appropriate therapy.'

Josh was checking the appointment book. He picked up the first file in his in-basket and then paused. 'I've got an excellent journal article on that subject. Lots of lovely pictures. Shall I hunt it out for you?'

'Oh, yes, please. Have I got a patient yet, Toni?'

Toni nodded. Her smile seemed relieved. 'She's on the phone but I expect she'll finish her call soon.'

Sophie looked puzzled and took another glance into the waiting room.

'Ding, *ding*! Nobody's dare, Mummy!' the toddler exclaimed indignantly.

'She doesn't look too sick.' Sophie smiled.

Oliver came down the corridor. 'Keep warm, lots of rest and keep up the fluids, Mrs Broadbent. You should feel much better in a few days.'

'Are you quite sure I don't need any antibiotics, Doctor?' Mrs Broadbent sounded disappointed. 'It's such a dreadful cough.'

'It's just upper airway congestion from your cold, as I explained.' Oliver didn't sound the least bit annoyed at having to repeat himself. 'Your chest is perfectly clear.'

'If you say so, Doctor.' Mrs Broadbent sniffed ungraciously and went through the archway to appear on the other side of the counter.

Oliver let Janet out of the office area, before entering.

'Mr Smythe?' Janet called. 'You can go now. It's been twenty minutes since your flu shot. Are you still feeling OK?'

'My arm's bloody sore,' Janet's patient grumbled loudly. 'And I'm late for the dentist now.'

Janet's soothing comment was lost as Toni spoke to Josh. 'Deborah has rung twice this morning already. I think she wants to make sure you don't forget about your usual lunch date.'

'God, no!' Josh's face creased with alarm. 'Tell her I'm unavailable, Toni.'

'For lunch?'

'For life.'

Oliver grinned. 'Friday night wasn't great, then, I take it?'

'Friday night was fine,' Josh said heavily. 'It was terrific until Debs said it.'

'Said what?' Sophie was amused by Josh's over-done hunted expression.

'The "M" word,' Josh intoned. His eyes widened in mock horror.

'Money?' quipped Oliver.

'No.' Josh looked at his partner solemnly. 'Marriage.'

Toni's smile looked rather satisfied. 'That's it for her, then,' she said crisply. 'Cross Debs off the list.'

Josh edged past Oliver, leaning over the counter briefly. 'June? You can come through now.' He glanced back at Toni. 'If she rings again, tell her I've skipped the country or died of flu or something.'

'Why don't you just tell her the truth?' Oliver suggested. 'You'll save everybody a lot of heartache if you're honest about it. Ask Sophie what she thinks about men who can't commit themselves. She's put me straight, I can tell you.'

Sophie looked away from her colleagues quickly. 'Mrs Chaplin? Would you like to bring Samantha through now?'

The toddler grabbed the phone and clutched it to her chest. *'No!'* she shrieked. *'Ding! Ding!* It's Daddy!'

One of the flu patients groaned audibly. Josh ushered his patient down the corridor. Oliver was shaking his head. 'Tangled webs,' he muttered sadly.

'Yes.' Toni sniffed delicately. 'And I'm the spider who's left to deal with the flies.'

'Let him sort out his own problems,' Oliver advised. 'Maybe then he'll make a fresh start. Like me. Life's quite simple when you sort out what it is you really want.'

'Hmm.' Toni was looking at Oliver curiously. 'You look like you have something new in your life.'

'I'm going away for the weekend,' Oliver announced. 'Hanmer Springs. Hot pools, forest walks, great food. I can't wait.'

Sophie was now standing in the archway, trying to concentrate on Mrs Chaplin's struggle with parting her daughter from the telephone. Samantha was getting alarmingly red in the face.

'You can bring the telephone with you, Samantha,' she offered. 'Maybe Daddy will ring you in my office.' She had missed Toni's comment on Oliver's enthusiastic announcement. Now he was speaking again.

'Would I go somewhere that romantic alone?' He was grinning suggestively at Toni but his eyes moved to catch Sophie, who had been unable to stop herself staring as she waited for her patient. Samantha was now dragging the phone along by the receiver, its curly cord stretched straight by the weight of the phone bumping along behind. It collided with the feet of the flu sufferer who had already been heard to groan. The man slumped back in his seat, covering his face with his hands.

'How 'bout you, Sophie?' Oliver asked brightly. 'Got any trips to Auckland planned?'

'No.' Sophie's response was curt. She could see Toni watching Oliver with a faintly stunned expression. Sophie moved away hurriedly. She wasn't interested in Oliver Spencer's plans for the weekend. Neither was she remotely interested in finding out the identity of his proposed companion. She could guess that easily enough. It wasn't jealousy she was feeling. That dull ache in her chest was probably just disappointment that Oliver was able to forget his physical attraction to her and transfer his attentions with such ease. Oliver Spencer was reverting to type. Publicly. No wonder Toni was looking stunned. She already had to deal with the fallout from one playboy's social calendar. Now she might have to deal with two.

It wasn't Sophie's problem, thank goodness. Right now she only needed to deal with Samantha Chaplin's glue ear and her mother's conviction that it was causing all her behavioural difficulties. The rest of the morning seemed to be taken up with feminine worries. Elderly Mrs Smithers had stress incontinence. Nineteen-year-old Claire was embarrassed by a nasty dose of thrush, and two women came in for their regular Pap smears. As the only female GP at St David's, Sophie knew she was likely to get more than her share of such cases, but that was fine by her. She would choose to see a female GP herself under similar circumstances.

Sophie's last task for the morning was to write out a promised prescription for some more antibiotic eye-drops for Toni who was using them as part of her post-eye-surgery care programme. The practice manager was already on her lunch-break so Sophie took the prescription down to the staffroom.

'I hope you haven't run out. I meant to do this first thing,' Sophie apologised. 'How is your eye?'

'No problems at all.' Toni tapped the lens over her left eye. 'I've had this lens changed to plain glass and I can see brilliantly. I'm going to book in for getting my other eye done as soon as possible.' She reached for the prescription. 'Thanks a lot, Sophie. I'll get this filled when I go down to the bank.' She smiled at Sophie. 'Have you got time for a coffee? I haven't asked but I've been dying to know how things are going with you and Greg.'

'They're not.' Sophie shrugged lightly and reached for a coffee-mug. 'Greg's found another woman.'

'What?' Toni looked aghast. 'How could he? What a creep!'

'I wouldn't say that exactly.' Sophie couldn't help but feel comforted by Toni's outrage on her behalf.

'I would,' Toni declared. 'Men are all the same, aren't they? And they have the nerve to blame women when things go wrong.'

Sophie thought of Oliver's proposed weekend away. She was about to concede that Toni might well have a point when Josh entered the staffroom, closely followed by Oliver.

'How could you do it to me, Toni?' Josh demanded sternly.

Toni gave Sophie a conspiratorial smile. 'Do what, Josh?' she asked innocently.

'Book Mr Collins in for my 2.30 appointment. It's Oliver's turn again, isn't it? I saw Mr Collins last week when he had that headache and was convinced he had a subdural haematoma.'

'Was that before or after the suspicious lymph node that turned out to be a boil?' Oliver grinned.

'It's your punishment,' Toni told Josh calmly. 'He rang just after I got an earful from Deborah on how she wasn't going to stand for jumped-up secretaries who were obviously trying to block contact between people who had important business to discuss.'

'Oh, God. Sorry, Swampy.' Josh looked contrite. 'OK. I won't complain about Mr Collins.' He sat down and grinned at Oliver. 'That is,' he added, 'unless he's carrying another jam jar.'

'The last one's still in the fridge.' Sophie stared disapprovingly at Oliver. 'I've never seen anything so disgusting. Janet reckons it's a bio-hazard and it's time you did something about it.'

'Right.' Oliver opened the fridge, grabbed the jam jar and dropped it into the open rubbish bin on the floor. 'Consider it done.'

Janet entered the room just as the jar landed with an impressive thud. Her eyebrows shot up. 'What was that?'

'Mr Collins's jam jar.' Sophie sounded just as surprised as Janet.

'You can't do that,' Janet told Oliver. 'It's a bio-hazard. From what I saw before the mould took over, it probably needs a lead casing.'

'Hardly.' Oliver laughed. 'And there's plenty more where that came from.'

'I'm sure there is,' Toni said dryly. 'Maybe Josh will get a replacement this afternoon.'

'What *was* it?' Sophie felt compelled to ask.

'Some sort of a toadstool,' Oliver responded. His dark grey eyes were dancing with amusement. 'Mr Collins found it growing in his veggie garden. He reckons it's tainting his cabbages and causing his problems with excessive flatulence.'

'Oh, please!' Janet was peeling the lid from her pot of yoghurt. 'I'm about to eat.'

'It's all right for you,' Josh said plaintively. 'I've got a 2.30 appointment with him.'

'Serves you right,' Oliver declared. 'Maybe Toni will forgive you for making her deal with the dreadful Deborah.' He winked at Toni. 'Put Mr Collins in the side room. It's a lot smaller than Josh's office.' He pointed a warning finger in Josh's direction. 'Just be careful not to light any matches.'

Sophie had to laugh. It was more than she would have done when she'd first arrived at St David's. The idea that dealing with the more difficult patients like Mr Collins could be seen as having entertainment value had been a little unnerving at first. Over the months, however, Sophie had come to understand the shared bond between the staff that might provide amusement privately at a patient's expense but allowed them to offer their patient the attention and interest he demanded without it becoming a tiresome burden. It was usually Oliver who could see the funny side first. In fact, it had been his sense of humour that had attracted Sophie before anything else.

Sophie's smile faded rapidly. She tipped out the rest of her coffee. 'I'm going to be late for this tutorial if I don't get moving. I'll see you all later.'

The tutorial on otoscopy was extremely worthwhile. Sophie had already had three occasions on which to use her new-found level of skills by Friday morning. Her second to last patient for the morning was an eight-year-old girl who'd had recurrent ear infections since infancy.

Sophie angled the speculum of her otoscope carefully upwards and forwards, having seen the junction of the posterior canal wall skin and the eardrum. She remembered the tutor describing the lateral process of the malleus as looking like a knuckle or a flexed knee and commenting that it was by far the most useful and reliable landmark on the eardrum. Sophie identified it with satisfaction and then ran through the rest of the six landmarks as she found them.

'Are you good at popping your ears, Katy?' Sophie queried. 'By pinching your nose and blowing hard?'

'I think so.'

'Good girl. Try it for me now.' Sophie watched to see whether a bulging of the eardrum would signify good Eustachian tubal function. It didn't.

'Right.' Sophie removed the speculum from the girl's ear. 'There's no sign of an active infection but the drums are looking very dull. We'll do a tympanogram and compare that to the one we did last month. Do you think you're having any trouble hearing the teacher at school at the moment, Katy?'

'No.'

'She never hears me when I tell her to tidy her room,' Katy's mother declared with a smile. 'She's as deaf as a post then.'

'I'll just go and get the tympanometer,' Sophie told them. 'Back in a minute.'

She went to the treatment room to collect the piece of equipment she needed. Janet was hanging up her wall phone. 'Fifteen recalls for repeat blood tests,' she sighed. 'Now I've got to start on all the preschool vaccinations coming up.'

'Poor you,' Sophie sympathised. She looked around. 'I need to do a tymp on Katy's ears.'

'It's over there.' Janet pointed. 'Beside the autoclave.' She ticked the last name on her list and reached for another computer printout. 'I should have had these appointments made by Tuesday,' she muttered. 'I don't know how I've got so far behind. By the way, you've got Ruby Murdock sitting in the waiting room.'

'I know. She's my next patient.'

'Her daughter's come with her.'

Sophie caught the amused inflection in Janet's voice. 'And?' she prompted.

'And they're sitting with two empty chairs between them, both looking like thunder.'

'Oh, help,' Sophie groaned. 'Thanks for the warning.' She gripped the tympanometer. Maybe the few minutes it would take to complete Katy's ear examination would be long enough for the dust to settle between Ruby and her daughter.

When Sophie followed her young patient out a good ten minutes later, however, she could see that the situation was unchanged.

'Mrs Murdock? I'm ready for you now,' Sophie said, not quite truthfully.

Ruby heaved herself out of her chair with some difficulty. She was wheezing heavily. Felicity King continued staring at the floor.

'Did you want to come in, too, Felicity?' Sophie asked casually.

'I suppose I'd better.' Felicity stood up reluctantly and Sophie's heart sank further at her grudging tone. It looked like this would be a far from easy consultation.

It turned out to be far worse than Sophie had anticipated.

'You're not sounding too good today, Mrs Murdock.' Sophie had her hand on Ruby's wrist as she sat her patient down. 'Have you used your Ventolin inhaler?'

'No.' It was Felicity who spoke. 'She says it doesn't help. She hasn't been using her Flixotide inhaler either or monitoring her peak flow.' Felicity was looking directly at Sophie, ignoring her mother. 'I only found out this morning.'

Sophie was frowning. Ruby's pulse rate was 130. She moved to her cupboard and withdrew an inhaler. Flipping it open, she gave it a good shake, watching Ruby's respiration rate as she did so. Her patient was breathing very fast and the muscles on her neck looked strained.

'That's because you haven't...been near me for three days.' Ruby had to take another breath in the middle of her sentence.

'Breathe out, Mrs Murdock,' Sophie instructed. 'As deeply as you can.' She held the mouthpiece of the inhaler in position. 'Now breathe in.' Sophie depressed the medication canister to release the bronchodilator.

'I got sick of the arguments, Mum,' Felicity said angrily. 'Just like I'm sick of the extra workload. I've got enough to do with three kids and a husband to look after.'

'They're his kids, too,' Ruby shot back. 'He's as lazy as they come... Look at the fuss he makes when...I ask him to mow my lawns.' Ruby's breathing was becoming more distressed as she forced her sentences out. 'I'm your *mother*, Felicity... Or doesn't that count for anything these days?'

Sophie was still frowning. Felicity mistook her expression for criticism and became defensive.

'For God's sake, Dr Bennett. All I did was remind

Mum that she'd promised to walk to the supermarket every other day for her exercise. It's only ten minutes away from her house, if that. It would save me giving up an afternoon once a week and it might even improve her health.'

'It was the *way* you said it,' Ruby puffed unhappily.

Sophie lifted her stethoscope from Ruby's back. She was horrified to see tears forming in the older woman's eyes. Her breathing was still deteriorating.

'Don't get upset, Mrs Murdock. We'll sort things out.' She gave Felicity a warning glance. 'I don't think this is a good time to go into it all. I'm a bit worried about this asthma attack.'

Neither woman seemed to hear her.

'There's a very easy answer to it all...and you know that...perfectly well.'

'You can't move in with us, Mum. I've told you it wouldn't work. Brent won't have it. He'd leave me. It's not fair to expect it. I'm doing all I can.'

'Not any more,' Ruby gasped. There was a bluish tinge to her lips that made Sophie step in more firmly.

She leaned down to make sure Ruby could see and hear her and she spoke loudly. 'I'm going to take you into the treatment room, Mrs Murdock. I think we need to start a nebuliser to get your breathing under control. I'm going to get one of our other doctors to look at you as well. Felicity, could you take your mum's other arm and help me, please?'

'Is she that bad?' Felicity looked alarmed. 'I thought she was putting it on—trying to make me feel guilty. It wouldn't be the first time and she's been upset ever since Monday when we talked about her wanting to move in with us.'

'This way,' Sophie ordered, ignoring the subject. 'Janet, can you set up a Ventolin nebuliser, please?'

It was ready by the time Sophie had Ruby propped up on pillows on the bed. The medicated mist filled the oxygen mask, pushed through the attached container by the flow of oxygen from a portable cylinder.

Sophie kept her fingers on Ruby's pulse and kept up a constant stream of verbal reassurance which she broke only to ask Janet to fetch either Oliver or Josh. Felicity stood at the end of the bed, looking very distressed.

'I'm sorry, Mum. I'm really sorry.'

Sophie felt a familiar wave of relief when Oliver entered the treatment room and calmly took charge of the situation. She could cope with anything as long as she had Oliver by her side. Felicity was sent to the waiting room. Janet squeezed another dose of Ventolin into the nebuliser mask and Oliver took Ruby's blood pressure and listened to her chest with his stethoscope. Then he patted Ruby's hand.

'I'm going to put a little needle into the back of your hand, Ruby,' he told her. 'Just in case we need to give you some stronger medicine.' He smiled reassuringly at Sophie. 'Set up an IV, would you, please, Sophie?'

Sophie was glad of the simple task. Severe asthma attacks were alarming for the doctor as well as the patient, she decided. It was an effort to remain calm to outward appearances. Ruby's breathing sounded a little quieter now. Did that mean she was improving or getting worse rapidly? A silent chest in a severe asthma attack was a serious sign.

Oliver swabbed the back of Ruby's hand and deftly slipped in a butterfly cannula, despite the fact that

Ruby's hand was shaking badly. Sophie had to admire his skill. She doubted that she could have gained IV access so easily. Oliver didn't seem at all worried.

'You're doing really well, Ruby. We'll get this under control in no time.' He looked across the bed at Sophie. 'Ruby's not on oral corticosteroid therapy, is she?'

'No. She has Flixotide and Ventolin inhalers.' Sophie found she could remember every detail of Ruby's file now that she had relaxed. 'Her best peak flow rate is around 340.'

'Good. We'll check that soon.' Oliver smiled at Ruby again as he picked up her wrist to check her pulse rate. 'How does your breathing feel now, Ruby? Any better?'

Ruby Murdock nodded, her eyes fixed gratefully on Oliver. He put her hand down, gave it another reassuring pat and turned to Sophie.

'I think she's settling.' Oliver hooked his stethoscope around his neck. 'I'll leave her in your capable hands. Keep an eye on things for a while. Watch her respiration and pulse rate and do a couple of peak flows over the next half-hour or so. I won't be far away if you need me.'

'Thanks, Oliver.' Sophie suspected she looked as grateful as Ruby Murdock.

'Any time.' He slipped Sophie the ghost of a wink. 'You would have managed just fine without me around, you know.'

The praise warmed Sophie. She could almost believe it, though she knew it would take her years to acquire the skill and confidence that Oliver Spencer demonstrated so casually. She had been impressed by his professional abilities from the first day she had

started at St David's and her admiration had only
grown since then. Dr Spencer was an impressive phy-
sician—exactly the type of doctor Sophie hoped to
become. She turned back to her patient.

'Let's try and do a peak-flow reading,' she said encouragingly. 'That way we'll be able to measure how
fast you're improving.'

Ruby was improving, but it was well over an hour
before Sophie was happy to stop watching her. Oliver
had gone on with his list, working through his lunch-
hour to make up for lost time. Sophie had no patients
for the afternoon which had been set aside as a study
period this week. She knew that Janet was finding it
awkward, seeing her patients in the side room, but
nobody wanted to send Ruby home too quickly.

'You're looking much better,' Sophie told Ruby
finally. 'How do you feel?'

'Terrible.' Ruby lifted the oxygen mask. 'Is Felicity
still here?'

'I'm not sure,' Sophie replied. 'I think she might
have gone to collect Laura from kindy.'

'Oh, dear. I need to apologise.' Ruby lay back
against her pillows and closed her eyes. 'I know I
can't move in with them.' She opened her eyes again
and looked sadly at Sophie. 'It's just that I'm so
lonely since my Arthur died.' Ruby struggled for control and Sophie passed her a box of tissues.

'I knew I was making life difficult for her. I think
I wanted Brent to leave and then maybe Felicity
would need me as much as I need her.'

Sophie listened patiently. The asthma attack was
under control. She had nobody waiting. Ruby could
take as long as she liked.

Janet poked her head around the door. 'I need to grab some vacutubes and things for a blood test.'

'Come in, Janet.' Sophie stood up. 'Ruby's much better. I think we could take her butterfly needle out and then we could go into the side room for a while.' She smiled at her exhausted-looking patient. 'How would you like a nice cup of tea, Mrs Murdock?'

'That would be lovely, dear. And why don't you call me Ruby? The other doctors here do.'

'Let me help you, then, Ruby.' Sophie smiled a little shyly as she collected the oxygen mask and lifted the tubing clear. It was a small thing, but Ruby's acceptance of her position alongside Josh and Oliver meant a lot. She was a part of the St David's team. One of 'the doctors'. Maybe she would follow the others' example and stop bothering to wear a white coat to advertise her credentials.

The good feeling lasted through a weekend that Sophie put determinedly to good use with some in-depth studying. She wanted to fly through her exams at the end of the year and earn her GP registration. Now, more than ever, she knew it was where she belonged.

Ruby Murdock *was* an excellent example of a general practice patient and not simply because of her collection of common medical problems. The complexities of relationships and their effects on everybody involved were a vital factor to be considered in treatment.

Who would have guessed how devoted Ruby had been to her husband and daughter, to the exclusion of ever forming a support network of her own. It hadn't even been obvious after Arthur's unexpected and fatal heart attack. It had been the broken ankle that had made Ruby realise just how alone and vulnerable she now was. And the fear had set in, making her cling to her daughter and use her progressive medical conditions as an emotional bind.

Sophie had talked little and listened a lot on Friday afternoon. When Felicity had come back to collect her mother, the discussion had continued for another hour. Maybe things wouldn't come right all at once but there was a lot out in the open and both Ruby and Felicity desperately wanted an improvement.

Had she seen Ruby Murdock as an inpatient in a hospital ward, Sophie would have concentrated on treating the presenting disease. Taking a holistic approach simply wouldn't have been feasible. It needed time to build up a rapport with her patient and with her patient's family. Had she been at St David's for as long as Josh, or even Oliver, she might have known Ruby's husband, shared the joy the birth of her grandchildren would have brought and spotted the danger signals of Ruby's decline far before they hit crisis point.

Sophie felt quite inspired by Monday. She was looking forward to the trivia and bustle of the new start to the week. She was also looking forward to sharing how she felt with Oliver. He was the only person who would really understand the new insight Sophie had gained. Imagine how her father would react. Or even Greg. Maybe Josh would recognise it but, much as Sophie liked and respected St David's senior partner, she felt that he was skating through life at a level far too superficial for her liking. Oliver had more depth. He was capable of, indeed actively displayed, the kind of skill and commitment to his career that Sophie now aspired to.

She felt badly let down when she met Oliver in the car park when she arrived for work.

'God, I don't feel like getting into a Monday,' he complained. 'The weekend was way too short.'

Sophie's desire to share her new-found confidence in her career direction evaporated. 'You had a good time, then?' she asked with forced brightness.

'Good!' Oliver grinned broadly. 'Good doesn't come anywhere near it. It was great! Fantastic! Memorable! Absolutely...' He searched for a new superlative.

Sophie snatched up her bag and slammed her car door shut. 'I hope that your companion was equally satisfied.'

Oliver pursed his lips thoughtfully. 'I didn't hear any complaints.'

Sophie stalked ahead of Oliver. 'I'm sure you didn't,' she muttered under her breath. If the kiss she had experienced was any indication of Oliver Spencer's prowess in the bedroom, *she* wouldn't be complaining either.

Oliver caught up with her by the time Sophie reached the wheelchair ramp. 'You know, you might be wrong about me, Sophie.'

'Really?' Sophie asked waspishly. 'In what way, Oliver?'

Oliver smiled cheerfully and held the door open for her. 'I might not be just the same as other men. I think I'm beginning to share your ideals about commitment. About the things that are really important in a relationship.'

'Congratulations.' Sophie allowed herself to sound reluctantly impressed. 'I suppose the next thing we'll hear about will be your wedding plans.'

Oliver looked surprised. Then he looked serious. 'Do you know, Sophie Bennett, that's another very good idea you've had? Tell you what. Let's make a deal. Let's swap invitations.' He leaned closer. Sophie could feel the warmth of his breath on her face as he spoke. 'You invite me to your wedding. And I'll invite *you* to *mine*.'

CHAPTER SEVEN

WEDDING invitations were the last thing Sophie Bennett wanted to think about.

Plans for her own wedding had always formed a delightful part of the fantasy of her future that Sophie had conjured around her relationship with Greg. A traditional ceremony, a beautiful dress—a wonderful occasion to mark the beginning of a lifelong partnership. She suspected that, along with the thriving general practice which had been intended to become the focus of their professional lives, there lurked a quaint cottage with a pram parked near the white picket fence. The death of her own plans were too fresh to have adequately scarred over. The thought of receiving an invitation to Oliver Spencer's wedding was much, much worse. Had he been serious?

It was impossible to ignore. Every time she saw him, Sophie had errant mental images of silver bells, doves and chubby cupids of the type printed on formal wedding invitations. Not that Oliver said anything more about the subject, but he exuded happiness. A blatant good humour on a par with Josh's typical, unhungover demeanour. A confidence about a positive outcome that filled Sophie with an unmistakable resentment. And, yes, she had to admit it— jealousy.

And he seemed to take every possible opportunity to rub it in. He was over-enthusiastic about minor things. Like when Sophie had told him that Ruby Murdock had joined a weight reduction clinic.

'Great!' He'd beamed. 'Fantastic!'

And Sophie had been instantly reminded of his satisfied appraisal of his weekend away with Christine Prescott.

'How's her asthma?' Oliver had queried with interest.

'Fine.' At any other time Sophie would have been delighted to have shared the progress. But her tone had been uncharacteristically offhand. 'She's using her preventative therapy consistently. She hasn't even needed her Ventolin for more than a week.'

Was Oliver setting out deliberately to try and make Sophie aware of how much she wanted him? Like always sitting as close as possible to her when they were in the staffroom together, or brushing her hand or arm if they happened to reach for stationery or patient files at the same time in the main office. Or leaning over her shoulder to discuss a patient's results. Sophie could prepare herself for the deliberate contact when Oliver gave her a tutorial or was demonstrating a new procedure or technique. It was the unexpected instances that were hard to handle. And there seemed to be far too many of them. Was he simply so happy in his own new relationship that he was unaware of the subtle change in his behaviour towards her? It was hardly sexual harassment, so why did Sophie *feel* so harassed?

Sophie tried to hang onto her new insight about how satisfying her career in general practice was going to be. She tried very hard not to let personal responses to her supervisor get in the way, but it was more difficult than she had expected. It took several days of effort before Sophie saw a glimmer of hope that her campaign had some hope of success.

Mrs Wentworth, a woman in her late sixties, had presented with a nasty rash on her face. Sophie had explored the possibilities of allergies and contact dermatitis from plants such as primulas or chrysanthemums, but it was the thick, flesh-coloured pair of stockings Mrs Wentworth wore that inspired a new tack. She was quite proud of her diagnosis when she got Oliver to check the prescription she had written.

'That should do the trick.' He nodded at her selection of steroidal cream. 'And a referral for prompt treatment of her varicose veins might help. What made you think of it?'

'We had a lecture at medical school on dermatology that stressed how important it was to look further than the presenting area of skin. I remember being impressed that someone's face could have a secondary reaction to gravitational dermatitis on someone's ankle.'

'Is the ankle badly affected?'

'Quite extensive scaling and inflammation over her left foot and ankle. Almost ulcerated in places. It'll take a while to get it sorted and she might need referral to a dermatologist, but hopefully this cream will help her face more quickly. I'll see her again next week.' Sophie smiled. 'It was an interesting case. I'm glad I got it right.'

'Dermatology can be very rewarding,' Oliver agreed. 'It's supposed to be the perfect specialty. Your patients never die, never get better and never get you up in the middle of the night.' His expression was deadpan but Sophie caught the gleam of lurking humour and the invitation to respond.

She smiled at the joke and then her smile broadened as she returned to her patient. Was it relief that she could enjoy Oliver's humour without a stab of pain at the thought of his wit being directed at eliciting Christine Prescott's giggles? That had to be some sort of progress.

Then Sophie had to ask Oliver to help her with a patient the next evening. Peter Phelps rushed in at 5.15 p.m.

'I can't stand it any longer,' he groaned to Toni. 'There's something in my eye and it's driving me crazy.'

Janet and Josh had gone at 5 p.m. Oliver was with his last patient so Sophie offered to help. Twenty minutes later she tapped on Oliver's door.

'He's got this lump of bark chip stuck to his cornea,' Sophie explained. 'It's quite obvious and the history doesn't raise any suspicion of a penetrating injury. He had a truckload of bark chip delivered for his garden and it was very windy. There's no sign of any subconjunctival haemorrhage.'

'Maybe he should go to A and E and have it checked. We don't have a slit lamp.'

'He's very keen to have it fixed now.' Sophie smiled wryly. 'It's his wedding anniversary and his wife's expecting to be taken out to dinner. I gather he forgot last year.'

'Oh.' Oliver grinned. 'On trial, then, is he?'

'I've instilled topical anaesthesia and tried to sweep it out with a cotton bud.' Sophie shook her head. 'The damn thing moves quite easily but it's stuck like glue.'

Oliver nodded. 'Foreign bodies can be astonishingly adherent to the surface of the corneal epithelium.' He jumped to his feet. 'Come on, I'll show you a trick.'

Oliver selected a fine 20-gauge needle, having examined Peter's eye. He made two bends in the needle, one at the bevelled tip and another halfway along its length.

'This means you can hold the needle parallel to the cornea,' he explained to Sophie. 'Much safer. You need to sweep the needle under the edge of the foreign body, using the side of the needle, not the tip.'

Sophie's hand shook very slightly as she positioned her hand. Oliver's hand closed gently over hers. 'Rest your little finger under the eye and steady the others on top. Hold the needle like a pen and keep the eyelid open with your other thumb. Don't blink, Peter.'

'I won't,' their patient promised. 'Do you think you can get it out now?'

Sophie found her hand quite steady with Oliver's support. She scooped the piece of bark chip onto the flattened end of the needle with a sideways motion and lifted it clear. Oliver clicked on his ophthalmoscope to check Peter's eye for any further debris.

'Clear as a bell,' he pronounced. 'We'll give you a quick vision check, some antibiotic drops to use for twenty-four hours, and put a pad on until tomorrow. You'll look like a pirate when you go out to dinner, I'm afraid.'

'As long as I get there,' Peter said gratefully. 'Thanks a lot.'

Oliver stayed until Sophie finished. 'Use a double pad,' he instructed her. 'Keep your eyes closed for the moment, Peter.' Oliver's hands remained in contact with Sophie's as she held the pads in place while he demonstrated an effective taping pattern.

Sophie was delighted to find that the physical contact this consultation had involved hadn't given her any kind of generalised physical reaction. She had been acutely aware of the touch of Oliver's skin on her own but the effect had been purely local. That was *definitely* progress. She even found herself thinking of someone other than Oliver Spencer as soon as he left the room. The patch on Peter's eye reminded her of Toni's campaign to get rid of her spectacles. The practice manager had been excited to receive an appointment to get her second eye done in a month or so and Sophie shared her pleasure at the prospect.

It didn't help that Oliver reported the next weekend as also being 'great' but Sophie held onto her own campaign. With the passing of another few days, Sophie found she had even discovered a way to stop those intense looks from Oliver Spencer's smoky grey eyes doing those peculiar things to her body. It was quite easy. All she had to do was look away in time. If the contact was curtailed after no more than two seconds or so, she was protected.

Sophie had it taped. She could cope. She had a sneaking suspicion that her tactic was annoying Oliver, however. His stare was becoming increasingly intense when she did catch his eye. Almost as though he was demanding the contact. It simply hardened Sophie's resolve. She was gaining a new emotional strength with every passing day. She wasn't going to let any preoccupation with what might have been distract her from her new focus.

The tutorial Oliver gave Sophie on reading ECGs the following week marked the second stage of a downturn which had been prompted by Oliver's satisfaction on the most recent 'fantastic' weekend. Dr

Spencer had appeared in Sophie's office, carrying a large plastic bag.

'Look what I dug up!' he told her happily. He reached into the bag and produced a handful of paper strips. 'I collected bits of every ECG I did as a house-man on my cardiology run. I've got hundreds of them.' He upended the bag on her desk, then picked one out at random. 'What's this?'

Sophie peered at the trace. 'Atrial flutter,' she said confidently. 'That's easy.'

'What's the rate?'

Sophie picked up her small ECG ruler and laid it against the trace. 'Atrial rate is 300,' she said. 'Ven-tricular rate is 150.'

'OK.' Oliver leaned over Sophie's shoulder. 'Show me the P waves.'

'There aren't any,' Sophie smiled. 'You've got F waves—flutter waves—instead.'

'Hmm.' Oliver sifted through the pile. 'I'd better find something more challenging.' He dragged a chair close to Sophie's and then sat down, continuing his search until he had two strips to spread out in front of Sophie.

'Tell me which is left and which is right bundle branch block and what causes the differences in the traces.'

Sophie concentrated hard. Oliver was an excellent teacher. The feedback on correct responses was en-thusiastic, and any prompting or correction needed was given without any hint of criticism. Sophie found she was thoroughly enjoying the session. So was Oliver.

'You know, this is a very timely refresher for me,'

he told her. 'Josh and I are just talking about buying an ECG machine for St David's.'

'Are you?' Sophie was startled. It wasn't a common item for a practice this size to own due to its expense and relative lack of everyday necessity.

'Our case load is going up all the time. Especially elderly patients. They don't appreciate having to go elsewhere every time they need an ECG and Toni doesn't appreciate having to chase up all the results.'

'I suppose not.' Sophie looked worried. 'You're not thinking of turning St David's into one of these new A and E clinics, with everything under one roof and patients being seen by a different doctor every time they turn up, are you?'

Oliver smiled. 'St David's is a family practice. Always has been and always will be. Some people like the new clinics. They don't have to wait around and they don't care whether the doctor they see knows them personally. They want to purchase their health care with minimum time and fuss. Supermarket medicine.' Oliver shook his head a little sadly but then smiled again. 'St David's will always be the corner dairy.'

'I'm glad to hear that.' Sophie sighed with relief.

'Why?' Oliver's glance was curious. And rather intense.

Sophie felt instantly on edge. How could he do that with just a look? Make her body wake up and shout an awareness of his proximity that was almost overpowering.

'It's because you feel the same way I do,' Oliver stated softly, not releasing their eye contact. 'Not many people do.' He smiled gently. 'Maybe you'd like to consider staying on after you get your registration. Josh and I have decided it's time to offer a third partnership at St David's.'

Sophie ran her tongue across her suddenly dry lips. Oliver's gaze flicked down and then returned. Sophie saw his eyes darken as his pupils dilated. So much for her campaign! The undercurrent was as strong as it had ever been, even though Oliver had set his immediate goals elsewhere. Did she want to have to try coping with that on a long-term basis?

'No way!' Sophie didn't realise she had spoken the instinctive reaction aloud until she saw the surprised disappointment on Oliver's face. It was too late to modify her response to something more appropriate to turning down an attractive professional appointment. And it was far too late for her to be sitting in a room alone with Oliver Spencer.

'I think I've had enough on ECGs,' Sophie announced a little breathlessly. She started collecting the paper strips.

'Are you sure?' Oliver made no move to help her. 'We haven't done much on second- and third-degree AV block.'

'I'm sure,' Sophie said firmly. 'Enough is enough.'

The downturn gathered pace and was capped off by a visit to St David's by Christine Prescott at the end of the week. Sophie was deliberately late for morning tea, unwilling to witness Oliver's presumed delight at Christine's arrival. The drug rep was the centre of attention from the rest of the staff by the time she did force herself to enter the staffroom.

'It's a really good new lipid-lowering product.' Christine's luxurious curls bounced around her face becomingly. 'Only once a day. The majority of patients are controlled by the lowest 10 mg dose.

Therapeutic response is evident within two weeks with a maximum response in four weeks.'

'Is that response maintained in long-term therapy?' Oliver asked around a mouthful of biscuit. Sophie eyed the remaining peanut brownies on the plate with distaste.

Christine nodded enthusiastically. 'Absolutely. The dose response study showed a reduction in total cholesterol of 35 to 50 per cent. LDL reduced in the range of 43 to 65 per cent and triglycerides by 20 to 35 per cent.' Christine smiled at Sophie. 'Have a muffin.' She pushed a plate of tempting-looking savoury muffins closer. 'Or a peanut brownie. Oliver says they're great.'

'No, thanks. I'm not hungry,' Sophie responded. She was watching Christine closely. She knew her subject all right. Probably had to be reasonably intelligent to field queries from the doctors. Like the one Oliver was asking, with great interest, about contraindications and drug interactions.

'There's the usual contraindication for lipid-lowering drugs in active liver disease, pregnancy and lactation,' Christine responded confidently. 'Clinical studies haven't shown any adverse interactions with anti-hypertensive agents. Digoxin levels have to be monitored, of course. Steady-state digoxin concentrations can go up by about 20 per cent. But, then, you would keep a careful eye on your patients' levels routinely.' Her glance at Oliver was admiring. 'You'll find this product comparable with or better than whatever you currently prescribe. The results are consistent in all forms of hyperlipidaemia, including patients with NIDDM.'

Sophie's interest quickened despite her inclinations. Ruby Murdock had non-insulin-dependent diabetes mellitus. She also had a high cholesterol level. If her diet didn't achieve control then she would need some drug therapy to reduce the increased risk she was running of heart problems.

'I'll leave you all the info,' Christine promised. 'And some samples. I'll look forward to hearing what you think next time I'm here.'

Josh was playing with the Swiss army knife emblazoned with Christine's drug company logo which must have been the gift of the day. He eyed Janet as she collected mugs and took them over to the sink. Then he eyed the knife beside Oliver. Sophie smiled as she saw Josh pick up both knives as he excused himself. One for each of the twins, no doubt. Josh Cooper was quite a softie about kids, no matter what he advertised concerning his own lack of interest in having a family.

The gesture on Josh's part and the delight she saw on Janet's face as Josh whispered in her ear and slipped the knives into her pocket chased away the unpleasant side of having to sit and watch Oliver Spencer and his girlfriend. Christine was packing up, sorting leaflets and samples into a pile for Oliver.

'I hear you had a great weekend, Christine,' Sophie said sociably. 'Fantastic, even.'

Christine gave her a startled look. 'What? Where did you hear that?'

Sophie merely raised her eyebrows and smiled knowingly. Christine's confused glance flicked over to Oliver who appeared to have spotted something of consuming interest through the window that overlooked the car park. She looked back at Sophie and shook her head enough to make her curls bounce again. 'I think you might have your wires crossed,' she said apologetically. 'It's *this* weekend I'm planning to really let my hair down.'

Oliver's attention snapped back. He licked his lips. 'That sounds very promising,' he murmured suggestively.

'I hope so.' Christine flicked the locks on her briefcase. 'The last few weekends really haven't been up to scratch at all.'

Sophie's jaw sagged. Just what sort of standard did the men in Christine Prescott's life have to aspire to? She sat in a slightly stunned silence as the drug rep left. Oliver hurried after her.

'Have you got a minute, Christine?' Sophie heard him ask casually. 'I'd like a quick word.'

'Sure, Oliver.' There was the sound of something being dropped and then Christine giggled. 'Ooh, thanks.'

'Come into my office.' Oliver also sounded amused. 'We'll have a bit more room. It won't take long.'

Perhaps that had been the problem, Sophie thought acerbically as she stalked past Oliver's firmly closed door seconds later. She gave the solid wooden panels a dirty look. Maybe that's why the last few weekends hadn't been up to scratch. Christine Prescott's fragile appearance probably disguised a rampant sexual appetite and stamina that few men could handle.

Sophie couldn't resist having a dig at Oliver when she passed him later that morning. 'Not up to scratch,' she said sadly. 'You'll have to try a bit harder, Oliver.'

'I intend to.' Oliver sighed happily. 'What a challenge! Practice makes perfect, of course.'

'Of course,' Sophie agreed. God, it was hard to smile convincingly when your jaws were clenched.

She felt like kicking something. Preferably Oliver. Perhaps it was fortunate that her next patient was Pagan Ellis. For the first time Sophie really felt confident that she could put an end to this nonsense of a birth in the surf. She wasn't going to allow this patient's forceful personality, however attractive, to persuade her into involvement with something she was far from happy about. If she wanted a water birth, fine. Hospital facilities still catered for what had once been a popular option.

'Sit down, Pagan,' she invited crisply. 'I'm delighted to see that you did go along for the scan.'

'It was cool. You were right,' Pagan said happily. 'The baby was really in tune with the ultrasound waves. It was moving around all over the place. The girl doing the scan said it was difficult to take measurements. It looked like it was trying to dance.'

Sophie wasn't going to be distracted by Pagan's fervent imagination. 'The estimated gestation according to size is about two weeks longer than you made it. That's quite a big difference. Are you sure of your dates?'

'Are you kidding?' Pagan's eyes were round with disbelief. 'This has all been planned by the stars down to the last *second*. I know when I conceived.'

'Are your periods always so regular?'

'How do you mean?'

'Well, if you always had a cycle of, say, twenty-eight days, then you could be fairly confident of ovulating at around day 14. If they varied then there's no way of really being sure when ovulation occurred. *Were* they regular?'

'Sometimes.' Pagan looked vague. 'If I got stressed out and forgot to keep up my meditation and stuff then they got a bit mucked up.'

'What's the shortest cycle you've ever had?'

'Oh, about two weeks, I guess.'

'And the longest?'

'I don't know.' Pagan looked bored. 'A couple of months, maybe.'

Sophie sighed and made a note.

'Look, it doesn't really matter, does it?' Pagan asked impatiently. 'I am pregnant now and that's what's important.'

'Exactly.' Sophie wasn't about to let Pagan start running this interview. 'I have a few concerns, the least of which right now is your exact delivery date.' She tapped her pen on Pagan's file. 'You've refused to have any blood tests. We don't know your blood group, which could be important if you needed a transfusion. We don't know your rhesus factor status. We don't even know your haemoglobin level. If you're anaemic, then the amount of oxygen carried to the baby will drop. It will slow its development.'

'It's already big.' Pagan sounded smug.

'It will also affect brain development,' Sophie continued. 'You're over sixteen weeks now so we should be doing an AFP test which can detect abnormalities such as spina bifida. You haven't been checked for the possibility of syphilis either. If you had it and you weren't treated before week twenty, it could be passed to the baby.' Sophie tapped her pen again. 'You haven't even provided us with a routine urine sample, Pagan. Protein detected in urine can be a useful sign of complications in late pregnancy. Sugar can indicate diabetes, which is one cause of having abnormally large babies. You haven't even supplied me with the name and telephone number of this midwife you've chosen.'

Pagan was looking round-eyed again. 'Boy, you really know your stuff, Sophie. I'm impressed. And that list!' She pointed to the paper Sophie had been tapping her pen against. 'Very Virgo.' She caught Sophie's stern look. 'Hey! Birth isn't an illness, you know. It's a perfectly natural event. Plenty of women have produced babies in the wilderness totally unaided.'

'Most of them weren't having their first baby at thirty-seven,' Sophie pointed out calmly. 'And plenty of them died.'

'I let you do an internal examination and take a smear,' Pagan said indignantly. 'You've taken my blood pressure and weighed me. I'm doing my bit. I just want to do it my way.'

'Well, you've got to let me do some things my way,' Sophie said firmly. 'Otherwise I'm going to have to ask one of the partners here to take over for me.'

'You can't do that.' Pagan shook her head. 'I checked. There's a government paper on consumer rights within the health and disabilities services. I have the right to be provided with the services that take into account the needs, values and beliefs of my cultural, religious, social or ethnic group.'

It was Sophie's turn to look dumbfounded.

'Look,' Pagan said kindly. 'If it's so important to you I'll have a blood test. OK? I'll let you test my urine.'

Sophie smiled stiffly. 'That sounds like a good start.'

'What else did you want to do today?'

'Janet, our practice nurse, will take care of things like your weight and blood pressure. I would like to check the fetal heart beat and your abdominal measurements.'

'That's cool.' Pagan looked amenable. 'Anything else?'

'I'd like to contact your midwife.'

'Oh.' Pagan shrugged and looked wistful. 'Actually, we've had a bit of a falling out. She came to the conclusion that I should have a water birth in a hospital. Can you imagine? Some ghastly unhygienic bathtub that's already been used countless times.'

'I'm sure they get sterilised at frequent intervals,' Sophie said wearily. It clearly wasn't a good time to admit that she'd had the same brainwave. 'Come and hop up on the bed, Pagan. I'll just get the fetal stethoscope.'

She met Oliver on her way to the treatment room. 'I can't win,' she complained. 'Pagan Ellis is throwing government regulations about health customer consumer rights at me now.'

'Put it all down on paper,' Oliver advised. 'Spell out the risks as bluntly as you like and leave a space for her to sign that she understands and takes full responsibility. Let her take it home and think about it for a week or two.'

'That's a good idea.' Sophie nodded. 'Maybe some common sense might sink in.'

'I'll help you draft out the document if you like,' Oliver offered. 'I'll have plenty of time over the weekend.'

'Really?' Sophie raised her eyebrows pointedly.

'What about the promising session with the hair being really let down?'

Oliver looked taken aback. The slip was momentary but it was quite enough to arouse a surprising flash of suspicion in Sophie.

'I'm sure I'll still have time,' he said smoothly. 'I haven't got *that* much stamina. How 'bout coming in for an hour or two on Saturday morning?'

'Sorry.' The thought of an hour or two alone with Oliver when he was preoccupied with building up stamina for the rest of the weekend wasn't attractive. 'I think I might head up to Auckland this weekend.' Sophie had the satisfaction of seeing another disconcerted flash in Oliver's grey eyes. 'Maybe next week.'

In fact, Sophie drafted the document herself over a weekend that had to have been the worst since she had terminated her relationship with Greg. She'd had no intention of leaving town but, having said that she might, she didn't want to be spotted out walking or shopping. Who knew where Oliver and Christine might choose to go in order to recover from their bouts of over-exertion?

'This is totally ridiculous,' Sophie told herself more than once. She didn't really know what was going on between them. Maybe they *hadn't* had such a good time in Hanmer Springs. Christine's indifference had been puzzling. But the thought of Oliver Spencer being less than truthful was unthinkable. And he was right. Just look at the misery Sophie had managed to create in her own life by being less than truthful. She'd done it again by suggesting that she might head to Auckland for the weekend. The thought had clearly bothered Oliver. But why?

At least having to write up a document for Pagan

to sign occupied an hour or two. Sophie dragged out her heavy obstetric textbook and listed all the complications of birth she could find that would be totally impossible to manage out of a hospital setting. Oliver would need to check it over. It might even need a medico-legal opinion, but Sophie eyed the completed draft with satisfaction. It should scare anyone into demanding that a high-tech obstetric unit be within easy availability.

High-tech. Sophie chewed her lip thoughtfully. Hadn't Pagan mentioned something about the Internet and the age of Aquarius being big on technology? Maybe that would be a more effective approach. Sophie made a trip to the local library late on Saturday afternoon. She returned home, armed with several books on astrology, which turned out to be a bonus by occupying her for a large portion of a cold, wet Sunday.

Oliver Spencer looked tired on Monday morning and was definitely less exuberantly cheerful. Sophie felt vaguely disgusted by this evidence of such an active weekend. She wished he hadn't bothered stepping into her consulting room to greet her.

'How was Auckland?' Oliver enquired politely.

'I didn't go after all,' Sophie said nonchalantly. She was through with being less than truthful. Completely cured.

'Really?' Oliver perked up. 'Why not?'

'Nothing to go for,' Sophie responded.

'Really?' Oliver repeated. 'That's a shame.' His tone didn't suggest any sympathy. 'So it's really all over between you and what's-his-name, then? No hope of a reconciliation?'

'No.' Sophie looked away and shifted papers on

her desk purposefully. 'I've drafted a document for Pagan Ellis to sign,' she said briskly. 'Maybe you could read it over and let me know what you think.'

'Sure.' Oliver was smiling, she could hear it in his voice. 'It would be a pleasure.' His eyebrows lifted encouragingly as Sophie glanced at him. 'Anything else I could help you with? I'm all yours.'

Yeah, right, Sophie thought acidly. Any moment now and Oliver was going to find a way to make this personal instead of professional. He just couldn't help himself. Did Christine find his charm as irresistible as Sophie once had? The thought of Christine galvanised Sophie into putting Oliver firmly back into his professional corner before he could step out of it any further.

'Actually, there is,' she informed him. 'I've got a tutorial and workshop on the management of hypertension coming up.' Sophie warmed to her purpose. 'I wondered if you might have a good basic textbook I could borrow.'

'Sure.' Oliver nodded slowly, as though accepting the reminder of his professional position as Sophie's supervisor. He nodded again. 'I could write you some exam-type, long-answer questions on the subject if you like. You might like to have a crack at them for practice.'

'Great.' Sophie checked her watch but Oliver didn't take the hint that it might be time to start work. She gave him a questioning glance. 'Was there something else?'

'I wish I'd known you hadn't gone to Auckland. I could have done with your advice.'

Sophie was rendered speechless. Oliver wanted her

advice? About what? The best way to keep Christine Prescott amused?

'I want to buy a house.' Oliver ignored the lack of response. 'I think it's high time I stopped renting. I want something a bit more permanent. I had a look at a few but I'm not sure. Should I go modern and low maintenance, do you think? Or something old with lots of character?'

Sophie cleared her throat. 'Try asking Janet,' she suggested coolly. 'She might be able to put you onto a real-estate agent.'

'Who, Dennis?' Oliver grinned. 'But Dennis is a dork.'

Sophie bit her lip to stop herself catching Oliver's smile. Damn it, they were contagious!

'I don't want a dorky house,' Oliver confided. 'I want something really special. Old, I think, and with a nice view. It has to have a big garden, too, with plenty of room for children to run around in.'

Suddenly it was easy not to smile. 'Just keep hunting, Oliver. I'm sure you'll find exactly what you want. It might even have a white picket fence in front of it.'

'Mmm.' Oliver finally turned away. 'Sounds perfect. I knew you'd have a good idea, Sophie. You're full of good ideas. I'll keep an eye out for that fence.'

Oliver Spencer was smiling cheerfully as he entered his own consulting room. The plan was proceeding far more effectively than he had hoped. The look in Sophie's eyes when he'd mentioned the garden—and children! She wanted it as much as he did. She just needed to realise that he was the person she wanted to share it with. Maybe it just needed one more little push—and Oliver knew exactly what might do it. Sophie Bennett wasn't the only person who could come up with good ideas.

CHAPTER EIGHT

IT HAD to be some sort of a nightmare.

Having spent so much time and energy trying to erase the images of weddings from her life, having successfully banished all the silver bells tied with satin bows—not to mention horrible, smug-looking cupids—Sophie couldn't believe she was being confronted by the real thing. The downturn had stopped. Now she had really reached rock bottom.

The images lay on the counter that separated the main office area from the waiting room. They were being perused with intense interest by Toni Marsh and Janet Muir.

'The cupids are really too much,' Toni decided. 'I love this dove with the wedding ring in its beak, though.'

'I prefer the frilly horseshoe,' Janet declared with a grin. 'It has to be good luck to get a man as far as an altar.' She sighed rather wistfully and then glanced up to see Sophie's stunned observation of the scene.

'Hi, Sophie. Did you order these samples?'

'*No,*' Sophie denied emphatically. 'Why would I do that?'

Toni's gaze was quizzical. 'Well, you're the only person around these parts who has been engaged. And Oliver did say you might be planning another trip to Auckland. We thought you and Greg might have made things up.'

Sophie sighed audibly. 'Greg and I haven't made

things up. I'm not going to marry him. I'm not going to marry anybody, and even if I was I wouldn't choose wedding invitations that looked anything like those.' Sophie gave the cards a disgusted glance.

'They got dropped off this afternoon by our stationery rep. Someone had rung in and asked for a selection.'

'They must have got the wrong medical centre.' Sophie shrugged. She gave the cards another cursory glance and repressed a shudder.

'Not at all.' Oliver and Josh appeared on the other side of the counter, both looking ready to head home. Oliver stepped closer to the display. 'I ordered them,' he said.

'You're joking!' Josh was eyeing the cards with the same expression he favoured for one of Mr Collins's jam jars. 'What the hell would you want wedding invitations for?'

'My wedding, of course.'

There was a heavy silence that lasted for several seconds. Then Josh reached out to lay his hand on Oliver's forehead.

'Afebrile,' he murmured. 'Very strange.'

'Get off.' Oliver grinned.

'You're not really thinking of getting married, are you?' Toni gasped.

'To tell you the truth, I've been thinking about it a great deal just lately,' Oliver confided. 'Someone told me quite recently that they didn't think I was capable of commitment. I'd like to prove them wrong.'

Josh shook his head with disbelief. 'How could you, Oliver? You've been there, done that.' He tried a disappointed look. 'I thought you were a man after my own heart. You told me yourself you had no intention of ever getting shackled again.'

'I didn't,' Oliver agreed seriously. 'It's funny how meeting the perfect woman can change your mind, though.'

Toni was nodding wisely. 'I knew you weren't a lost cause, Oliver.' She shot Josh a mildly triumphant glance. 'Unlike some people, whose names I won't mention.'

Josh sighed heavily. 'I give up. Spill the beans, then.'

Oliver shook his head. 'When the time is right I'll make an announcement, and I promise you'll all be very surprised.'

'Who is she?' Janet demanded. 'Do we know her?'

'I'm not telling,' Oliver said airily. 'I'm leaving it up to her to decide when to go public. I couldn't betray that trust.'

'But do we know her?' Janet persisted.

'Oh, yes.' Oliver nodded casually. 'I'd say you all know her pretty well by now.'

'You don't look very surprised, Sophie,' Josh observed. 'Do you know something we don't?'

'My lips are sealed,' Sophie said faintly. Then she summoned up a smile and shook her head. 'I probably know less than you do. After all, I haven't been here very long.'

'Seems like ages,' Josh commented.

'Gee, thanks,' Sophie said dryly.

'I mean I can't imagine the place without you now.' Josh took a last look at the invitations. 'Those cupids are disgusting.'

'Oh, I don't know.' Oliver scooped up the cards.

'They might grow on you. What do you think, Sophie? I'd really value your opinion.'

Sophie just gaped at him. She had no words available.

Oliver tidied the stack of cards by tapping the edges on the counter. 'I'm going to take these home. Some decisions are best made in private.' He winked at Sophie.

'Some decisions are best not made at all,' Josh said darkly. 'I don't know what's got into you, Oliver.'

'Love,' Oliver declared. 'You should try it, Josh. It's good for the soul.'

'So's chicken soup.' Josh followed Oliver out. 'I don't like that either.'

If the weekend spent wondering about what Oliver and Christine might have been up to had been bad, it paled in comparison to the empty hours of Monday evening. Sophie tried to tackle the work she'd carried home but looking at Oliver's carefully thought-out questions covering the topic of high blood pressure did nothing to lift her mood. Oliver had written the mock exam paper by hand. His writing had a very distinctive style. Clear and flowing. Confident but not flashy. An amusing quirk here and there. Rather indicative of Oliver's personality, really.

Perhaps a glass or two of Chateau Cardboard might provide some emotional shelter from the ominous black clouds Sophie could sense waiting. Maybe a good, brisk walk would let her endorphins dilute the hovering depression. The more attractive alternative of chocolate was unavailable so Sophie finally chose a long, hot soak in the bathtub. She gave herself a stern talking to after her stress levels had subsided slightly.

She had no reason to be jealous of Christine Prescott. None at all. She could have been with Oliver herself if she'd been that keen. It had been a conscious decision to turn down the opportunity of an affair with the man. She'd accused him of lacking commitment. Of being shallow. And hadn't he proved her correct by the ease with which he had shrugged off the physical attraction he had demonstrated for her in favour of the new delights of the drug rep?

Or had he?

What had Oliver meant about proving her wrong about being able to commit himself. Was it possible that Oliver had invented his relationship with Christine in order to make himself seem a more desirable prize? It would fit with Christine's odd reaction to her query about the weekend. But why take it further? As far as telling her he was hunting for a family home. As far as producing sample wedding invitations. Was he just flaunting the possibilities? Was Oliver, in fact, *trying* to make her jealous and goad her into competing with another woman?

If he was, then he was barking up entirely the wrong tree. Sophie Bennett wasn't interested in anything less than the real thing. A physical relationship on its own would never be enough. The man she chose would have to feel exactly the same way as she did. And if he did feel the same way there would be no question of having to compete. Sophie felt quite happy with the mental circuit she had just completed. She did *not* want an affair. What she wanted was…Oliver Spencer. Body *and* soul.

Sophie groaned aloud and hauled herself out of the

bath. She towelled herself dry with unnecessary vigour. Back to square one. So much for pure lust. Her soul had fallen in love with Oliver a long time before her body had transferred allegiance. She had fallen in love with his intelligence. His compassion. His humour. She had responded to those qualities from the day she had met Oliver. She hadn't anticipated the physical response and it had grown gradually enough for her to deny the implications. Ironically, it had been her respect for Oliver's integrity which had made her analyse her own feelings and had led to her breaking her engagement. But that had been as far as she'd had the courage to go.

An emotional coward, that's what she was, Sophie decided as she got ready for bed. If she'd had any strength of character she wouldn't have let her father upset her so repeatedly over the years. She wouldn't have coasted along in a relationship with Greg that couldn't have gone any further than a teenage romance. She wouldn't have worried about admitting her error of judgement to her colleagues. And she wouldn't have panicked at the thought of what havoc a relationship with Oliver Spencer could have wreaked in her life. So what if it had only been sexual in the beginning? A relationship had to start somewhere or it couldn't grow. What had she expected? That Oliver would vow undying commitment before he let her know he fancied her?

How stupid to have blamed Oliver for being the catalyst. He had done her a favour. By showing her that there was more available than a good friendship, he had pushed Sophie into performing the first courageous act in her entire emotional history. She had broken off an engagement that had lacked any kind of real depth. Sophie shook her head in disgust. She had even tried to reinstate it. If Greg hadn't already been otherwise occupied she might have bolted back into a future of trying to deny what she knew she might have missed out on.

What she *had* missed out on. At least as far as Oliver Spencer was concerned. He might have all the ingredients Sophie could wish for but he was lacking the most important one. He didn't share her view about the sanctity of a meaningful relationship. He had introduced more players to his team. Even the idea of marriage was a game and the playing cards were now wedding invitations.

Sophie's stream of negative thoughts had to be firmly shunted aside the next day, but the strain of maintaining a cheerful appearance between the welcome distraction of dealing with patients was enormous. Nobody seemed to notice how tense she was. They were all too busy speculating on what had come over Oliver and who the mystery woman might be. When Sophie found the staff had gathered for lunch and could talk of nothing else, she carefully distanced herself by sitting on the couch. She picked up a copy of *GP Weekly* and tried to concentrate on the article predicting an epidemic of hepatitis C.

'But who *is* she?' Janet queried desperately, standing beside the group at the table. 'At least give us a clue, Oliver. What does she look like?'

'Gorgeous,' Oliver responded promptly.

'Brunette or redhead?' Josh asked.

'Neither. She's kind of, well, blonde-ish.'

Sophie read the same sentence for the third time. The words were a little blurred.

'What does she do? Something medical?'

'Mmm. Definitely something medical.' Oliver was grinning. 'And that's all I'm saying.'

'Have you set a date for the wedding?' Toni asked hopefully.

'Not exactly.' Oliver sounded less confident. 'I haven't quite asked her yet.'

'You must be pretty sure she'll say yes,' Toni pointed out. 'Or you wouldn't have ordered those invitations.'

'I'm keeping my fingers crossed,' Oliver said wistfully. 'I just have to think of some way of proposing so that she'll know I'm serious and not just playing games.'

'If she's the right person for you, she'll know,' Toni said knowledgeably. 'And if she doesn't then it would probably not have worked out anyway.'

'And if it doesn't work out,' Josh said kindly, 'I'll let you borrow my little black book.'

'Little!' Toni's exclamation was scathing. 'What is it, volume fourteen?'

Janet moved to sit on the couch. 'You're very quiet, Sophie. Are you OK?'

Sophie nodded. She glanced at the first sentence of the article she still hadn't managed to focus on. 'The conservative estimate of people in New Zealand with hepatitis C is 40,000 and increasing steadily,' she told Janet with concern. 'It's an epidemic that's being largely ignored.'

'Mmm.' Janet was clearly not enthralled.

Neither was Sophie. She dropped the glossy paper and excused herself. At least she had a full afternoon clinic of patients to distract her. There was nothing when she arrived back at her empty house, totally exhausted but still not prepared to allow herself another bout of introspection and critical self-analysis. This time she headed straight for the wine cask. The only way out of all this was to do something really courageous. Like put it all behind her and move on. To find a substitute. Like a career. It hadn't been so long ago that the thought of general practice long term had been very inspiring. Maybe it would be enough on its own. Sophie nodded decisively and raised her glass in a private toast.

Maybe she could try for the third partnership at St David's. But what if Oliver was serious about Christine, which seemed like more of a definite possibility after the clues he had dropped today? Could she see and work with him every day? Receive that silver embossed invitation to his wedding? See photographs of gurgling little Spencers in pride of place on Toni's noticeboard? Not likely. No way!

A career at St David's as a substitute would have to be a temporary measure. A means of getting through a sticky patch. A focus that could allow the chaos of her emotional life to settle into some semblance of order. And preferably get buried. It had worked for a while as a means for getting her over what she had thought to be simply a physical obsession with Oliver Spencer. It could work as a means of starting again. She was at rock bottom after all. The only way now was up. It could work. It *had* to work. That test paper on high blood pressure was probably a good place to start. She would see if she could tackle it without noticing the handwriting or wallowing in images of the writer.

Sophie arrived at St David's on Wednesday with the strength of her new determination carefully maintained. She went straight to her own office, removed a manila folder from her bag and then marched purposefully two doors down the corridor. Oliver's door was open. He was browsing through a medical journal.

'Here's the assignment you set for me on the management of hypertension.'

'That was quick.' Oliver held out his hand for the folder. 'What did you do? Stay up all night?'

'Something like that,' Sophie muttered. She had caught sight of the wedding invitation samples, now spread out on the blotter that marked the central area of Oliver's large desk. '*I* didn't have any major distractions,' she couldn't help adding.

Oliver grinned. 'The cupids are cute, aren't they?'

'Gorgeous.'

'Now I'm trying to decide on a honeymoon destination.' Oliver seemed unperturbed by Sophie's sarcastic tone. 'A week in Fiji, do you think? Or maybe Norfolk Island?'

'I hear Hanmer Springs is very romantic,' Sophie said coolly. 'I guess it depends on how far you want to go.'

'Exactly.' Oliver's glance speared Sophie with unexpected challenge. 'How far do *you* want to go, Sophie?'

Sophie was spared having to respond to the odd query by the angry voice outside Oliver's door.

'I don't *want* coffee. And I *don't* want any bloody paracetamol.'

A door slammed and both Sophie and Oliver turned in dismay to see Toni walk past, a steaming mug in one hand, something curled in the palm of the other. She smiled wryly at her audience.

'Well, I tried.' She carried on towards the kitchen.

Sophie was still staring, as though she expected Josh to rush past the door on his way to apologise to Toni.

'Hangover, I expect,' Oliver said lightly. 'He looked a bit pale and his eyes were decidedly blood-shot this morning.'

'Really?' Sophie's tone was unsympathetic. 'And it's only Wednesday.'

'I think he's still having hassles, trying to get rid of Deborah,' Oliver mused. 'He should have taken my advice and been honest with her in the first place.'

'It must be nice to be right all the time.' Sophie could hear both of Toni's phones ringing. Maybe Janet was late this morning. The boys had been difficult to get off to school lately. Sophie sighed. 'I'd better go and answer those calls. I have a feeling it's going to be one of those days.'

Oliver picked up a large black bag that was beside his chair. 'Time I escaped, then. Half of the Bay Villa Rest Home is down with flu. It should keep me out of mischief all morning.'

Sophie kept ahead of him. 'Let's hope Josh gets his act together, then. I don't fancy having to cope on my own.' She ducked into the main office and reached for the phone. The other one had stopped ringing. Oliver paused briefly on the other side of the counter as she picked up the receiver. His smile was warm.

'You'll never have to do that, Sophie. Don't worry.'

'Hello?' A voice called faintly. 'Hello? Is anyone there?'

'St David's Medical Centre,' Sophie responded

automatically. She watched the front door swing shut as Oliver strode out. 'Sophie Bennett speaking.'

'Sophie? Oh, thank goodness. It's Pagan Ellis here.'

Sophie blinked. She wouldn't have recognised the voice.

'I feel awful, Sophie. Something terrible's happening.'

'Calm down, Pagan. What's happening? Are you bleeding?'

'No—I just feel terrible.'

'Can you come in? I haven't got anyone booked until 9.30. How soon could you get here?'

Pagan arrived at 9.15 by taxi. She looked pale and distressed. 'I'm so hot,' she told Sophie. 'I've got a splitting headache and I hurt all over. And I keep getting these contractions.'

'You've got a dose of flu.' Sophie told her a short time later. 'And you're running a high temperature. Have you taken any paracetamol?'

'God, no! I can't take any drugs,' Pagan moaned. 'It might be dangerous for the baby.'

'A high temperature might be more dangerous,' Sophie told her. 'I'll get you some in a minute. How long have you been noticing these contractions?'

'Since last night.'

'Are they painful?'

'No. It's the only bit of me that doesn't hurt.' Pagan was close to tears. 'Oh, I feel sick.'

'Have you timed the contractions at all?'

'Just before I rang you. I'm getting them every five to ten minutes.'

'I'm going to get Dr Cooper to come and have a look at you, Pagan,' Sophie told her gently. 'I'm really not experienced enough to deal with this on my own.'

Pagan seemed unconvinced of Josh's ability despite his thorough examination. He showed no signs of his earlier bad temper even when faced by Pagan's doubts.

'I'm only just twenty weeks pregnant. I'm not supposed to be going into labour,' she sobbed. 'I want to see a specialist.'

'Exactly what I was going to suggest,' Josh told her calmly. 'I don't think you're in labour, Pagan. Your cervix isn't effaced at all and you've been getting these contractions for some time. You're obviously unwell with what looks like a viral illness and it's making your uterus irritable. To be on the safe side, I think we should get you admitted to Women's and have the experts keep you under observation for a while.'

'Oh, yes, please,' Pagan whispered. 'Can I go now?'

Josh nodded. 'We'll call an ambulance for you.'

Sophie's first scheduled patient had to wait twenty minutes and Toni caught her attention as she grabbed the file.

'I've squeezed an extra one in for you at 10 a.m. Can you cope?'

'Sure.' Sophie could see that both Toni and Janet were stressed. It was definitely one of those mornings.

Whatever the level of stress being experienced by both the practice manager and the nurse at St David's, it was nothing to Sophie's reaction on discovering who her 10 a.m. appointment was with. Christine Prescott sat on the other side of Sophie's desk and smiled shyly.

'I hope you don't mind me coming here—as a patient, I mean.'

'Not at all.' Sophie endeavoured to make her smile welcoming.

'I don't really have a GP,' Christine explained. 'I travel so much, being a drug rep, but I'm giving up the job soon and I expect we'll be settling in Christchurch.' Christine's smile was almost embarrassed. Sophie understood why when her attention was caught by the twisting movement of Christine's fingers. Twisting that was directed to the ring on the third finger of her left hand.

Sophie swallowed, to try and ease the sudden tightness in her throat. 'You're engaged?' Her voice came out with a croak.

'Mmm.' Now Christine definitely looked embarrassed. 'And not a minute too soon, it would seem.'

'Oh?' Sophie wasn't even attempting a smile now. She could sense what was coming. Like the chill that descended when the black clouds of a southerly blast built up to breaking point.

'I'm pretty sure I'm pregnant.' Christine bit her lip. 'That's why I popped in. I want to be sure before I tell my fiancé.'

'Of course.' Sophie noticed the slight tremor in her hand as she picked up her pen. 'How old are you, Christine?'

'Twenty-two.'

'And do you know the date of the first day of your last period?'

'Not exactly. It's about five, no, probably six weeks ago.'

Sophie glanced at the calendar on her wall. About

two weeks before Oliver had been away to Hanmer Springs, then. That figured.

'Have you been using any form of contraceptives?'

Christine sucked in her breath. 'We did *try* to remember.' She glanced at Sophie appealingly. 'You get a bit carried away sometimes. You know how it is.'

'Mmm.' Sophie didn't know at all. She had never been carried away by an irresistible physical passion. Maybe she should have tried it. Maybe if she had it would be her with an engagement ring on her finger again and Oliver Spencer's baby starting to grow inside her. Sophie felt sick.

'We can do a urine test for you right now, Christine. It should be quite conclusive but we'll back it up with a blood test if necessary.'

Christine watched Sophie select the testing kit and a specimen jar from her cupboard.

'I feel a bit shocked, to tell you the truth. I'm not sure how my fiancé is going to feel about it.'

'It's always a bit of a shock if it's not planned,' Sophie said calmly.

'Oh, we're planning to have children,' Christine said confidently. 'It's just that we weren't planning on starting quite so soon.'

'Take this sample jar with you.' Sophie shoved it across her desk. 'The toilet's just opposite the main office, on the right as you go down the corridor.'

The rest of the morning passed in something of a blur for Sophie. Fortunately the patients had only minor complaints. She didn't go near the staffroom when she had finished. She had no appetite for lunch. She had no desire to attend the Wednesday afternoon tutorial session at the hospital either, but at least it allowed her to escape from St David's for a few hours.

Oliver was swinging his large, black bag as he sauntered in from the car park. Sophie tried to get past with just a chilly nod but Oliver didn't let her get away with it.

'I hope Josh's bad mood wasn't that contagious,' he called. 'I was planning to enjoy my afternoon.'

Sophie stopped in her tracks. How dared he be so cheerful? She supposed Christine hadn't contacted him with the news of her positive result yet. Would he *still* look so cheerful when he learned of his impending paternity?

'I'm sure you will.' Sophie met his bland gaze angrily. 'You might even get some good news. Maybe I should offer my congratulations in advance.'

'What?' Oliver was frowning now. 'What on earth are you talking about, Sophie?'

'I saw Christine Prescott this morning,' Sophie snapped. Rules about confidentiality didn't apply between doctors, did they? 'Nice ring, by the way, but you'd better get on with sending out those invitations.'

Oliver wasn't frowning now. He was staring at Sophie as though he'd never seen her before.

'And I wouldn't recommend the hot pools as a honeymoon destination,' Sophie added triumphantly. 'Not a good idea for a pregnant bride.'

The colour drained out of Oliver's face with remarkable speed. 'God, Sophie,' he said in a shocked tone. 'You don't really think that I—'

'I've got to go,' Sophie interrupted. 'I've got a tutorial on antenatal care to go to. Appropriate, wouldn't you say?'

'Sophie, listen.' Oliver's facial muscles were working overtime. 'Christine Prescott may very well be pregnant but—'

'She *is* pregnant,' Sophie interrupted again. 'Very definitely. About five weeks. She would have conceived about the weekend of—'

'But it's *not* my baby!' Oliver exploded. 'It *can't* be! Christine Prescott means nothing to me, Sophie. I've never even *touched* her. I've never wanted to!'

Sophie allowed a full two seconds' silence to tick past. 'Oh, Oliver,' she said sadly. 'And you were the one who convinced me how important honesty is. How important commitment is.' She shook her head and turned away.

'Shame on you, Oliver Spencer.'

CHAPTER NINE

THE large wall clock gave the time as being only 9 o'clock.

The first patient for the morning had yet to enter the premises but the St David's Medical Centre staff looked as if they'd already had enough.

Janet had rung in to say she'd be late. The boys were sick and the babysitter couldn't get there until 10 a.m. Josh seemed even grumpier than he'd been yesterday morning and now Toni was tight-lipped.

'All I did was ask if he was feeling any better,' Toni muttered indignantly to Sophie. 'He didn't have to snap at me.' She snatched the referral letter she'd just finished out of the computer's printer tray. 'Sometimes I wonder why I bother getting out of bed.'

Sophie nodded wearily. She had felt exactly the same way herself this morning. Or rather, she'd wondered why she'd bothered getting *into* bed, seeing as she hadn't had a wink of sleep. She'd been tortured by images of a cheerful-looking Oliver, a smug-looking Christine and gurgling little bundles that managed to look cheerful *and* smug.

She couldn't even remember precisely what the tutorial had been about yesterday afternoon. The expected antenatal subject had been postponed in favour of geriatric problems of various kinds. Sophie had gone off on a tangent then, too, imagining what her

166

own old age might be like. Lonely, probably, with maybe just a few cats for company. Like Toni…

'Sorry?' Sophie gave herself a mental shake. 'Did you say something, Toni?'

'Nothing worth repeating,' the practice manager told her gloomily. 'Did you get that message in your in-tray?'

'I haven't looked yet.' Sophie got up from the corner chair. 'I knew there was something I came in for.'

Toni answered the phone. 'Oh, hello, Mr Collins.' There was a long pause. 'Is that right?… *Have* you?… Goodness me!' Toni's pencil was hovering over the appointment book under Josh's name.

Catching Toni's eye, Sophie received a wink. She smiled and nodded. If anybody deserved a visit from Mr Collins this morning, Josh Cooper did. Sophie changed her mind as she saw Oliver hurry in through the front door. He looked even worse than she felt. His tie was crooked and he looked as though his chin hadn't had more than a very brief encounter with a razor. He also looked tired. Maybe a consultation with Mr Collins would perk him up a bit. Sophie tapped the name in the appointment book and then pointed to an empty space under Oliver's name. She raised her eyebrows questioningly at Toni. The practice manager looked at Oliver and frowned in concern as she continued talking smoothly.

'I'm sure you're right, Mr Collins, but you'll need to discuss it with one of the doctors. I'm really not qualified to…' Toni grimaced in frustration. 'Eleven o'clock,' she said firmly, clearly interrupting. 'Excuse me, Mr Collins, but my other phone's ringing.'

'Don't you dare send him in my direction,' Oliver

muttered. He cast a rather haunted glance at Sophie. 'What are you doing?' he demanded.

'I'm reading the fax from the O and G consultant who admitted Pagan Ellis yesterday. Looks like they've managed to get her temperature down and the IV salbutamol infusion has settled the uterine activity.' Sophie couldn't help smiling. 'Apparently, she's booked herself in to use the hospital's water-birth facilities in November.'

'I told you she'd see sense eventually.'

'So you did.' Sophie smiled blithely at Oliver. 'I can't think what I found to worry about.'

Oliver's face darkened perceptibly at the hint of mockery in Sophie's tone. Toni turned from talking to the woman at the counter who was holding a protesting toddler.

'Sophie, you couldn't take young Benjamin's stitches out, could you? Ben's mum wants to get him to day care and can't wait until Janet arrives.'

'Sure.' Sophie smiled at the woman. The small boy now lay sideways in her arms, kicking his feet vigorously. If she were Ben's mother she'd probably be keen to get him to day care as well.

'Take him through to the treatment room, Jean,' Toni directed. 'Dr Bennett will be with you in just a minute.'

'I'd like a word when you're through,' Oliver told Sophie. 'I tried to call you last night.'

'Did you?' Sophie watched Ben's mother give up the struggle to hold her son. She grabbed his wrist the moment his feet touched the floor.

'Come *on*, Ben. Nobody's going to hurt you.'

I wouldn't bet on it, Sophie thought. But hopefully it wouldn't be her.

'You were on the phone,' Oliver said accusingly.

'Well, actually...' Sophie hesitated. She had taken her phone off the hook last night. Her father often chose a Wednesday to make his duty call and he was the last person Sophie had felt like talking to. Well, almost the last. She gave Oliver a quizzical glance. How many times had he tried to ring her? And what about? Did the fact that she'd forgotten to replace the receiver until this morning have anything to do with the shadows under Oliver's grey eyes? How ridiculous. Sophie smiled again.

'I expect it was about my assignment,' she suggested blithely. Ben's feet were disappearing through the door of the treatment room. Backwards. His mother must have a grip under both armpits by now. Sophie knew it was time to offer assistance. 'I'm sure we'll get a chance to talk later, Oliver.'

'You can count on it,' Oliver said darkly. 'I'll be in my office as soon as you've finished filling in for Janet.'

The stitches Ben had needed above his eye, thanks to the jousting tournament with heavy sticks which he had instigated at day care, were quite tricky to remove. Sophie tried bribing him with a teddy-bear-shaped biscuit but, having endured the tweak of the first stitch coming out, Ben had every intention of keeping the other three.

Sophie considered asking Oliver to help but decided against it instantly. The thought of disturbing Josh was just as unappealing. Finally, she called Toni, who expertly positioned herself on a chair, the toddler on her lap, his arms crossed and his hands held firmly by Toni.

'That's great.' Sophie nodded approvingly. 'If you

just steady his head, Jean, this will only take a second or two.'

It took long enough for Toni to receive a couple of bruises to her shins and for her to have told Ben all about the secret supply of sweets she kept in the office. It also took long enough for the waiting room to get quite full. Sophie gave two people flu shots, took a blood sample for a digoxin level and then smiled as Ruby Murdock came into the treatment room. Ruby was wearing a bright pink tracksuit and white trainers.

'I've just come for my BP check and to have my weight done,' she told Sophie. 'I wasn't expecting to see you, dear.'

'I'm being Janet for a while,' Sophie explained. 'She's a bit late this morning. 'You're looking great, Ruby.'

'I've lost seven kilos,' Ruby said proudly. 'I walked over here this morning. It took thirty minutes.'

'Good on you.' Sophie wrapped the BP cuff around Ruby's arm. 'How's the asthma?'

'Much better. In fact, I feel much better generally.'

'That's great.' Sophie listened for a moment, then removed her stethoscope. 'Your BP's down a bit, too. How's Felicity?'

'Good.' Ruby smiled at Sophie. 'She's taken up yoga. I look after Laura for her on Tuesday afternoons. She says it's just what she needs. I've got someone in to help me with the housework and I'm getting all my food through the weight clinic. I think things are improving all round, really.'

'I'm so pleased,' Sophie said warmly. 'Keep it up. I'll just do a quick blood sugar and cholesterol check while you're here, too.'

Sophie was labelling the blood sample a minute later when Janet finally arrived.

'I'm so sorry I'm late,' she apologised. 'You're going to be rushing all morning to catch up with your own appointments now.'

'Not to worry.' Sophie smiled. 'My first is Mrs Wentworth. She's usually late and then goes to sleep in the corner. I don't think I ever rush as much as you do. I feel like I've done a day's work already. How do you stand the pace?'

Janet grinned. 'It's a breeze compared to being at home with two children. Just wait. You'll find out what real work is one day.'

Sophie's smile was wistful. Would she? Would she ever have to cope with the challenge of juggling a career with motherhood? Which one would be more fulfilling in the long run? Probably motherhood. Sophie suppressed a sigh. What had happened to that wonderful determination to focus on her career? Her fragile mood was in danger of cracking again and it sounded as if she might not be the only one having difficulties. Sharing an anxious glance with Janet, Sophie stared at the door. She could hear Josh's quiet but unmistakably angry voice. He was standing outside the treatment room door, presumably talking to Toni.

'I said there's no way I'm seeing him. I'm the senior partner here, Toni. If I say Oliver sees him, then Oliver sees him.'

Janet followed Sophie into the main office. 'It's my fault for being late,' she said mournfully. 'I've caused all sorts of problems, haven't I?'

'It's not you causing the problems around here,' Toni responded crisply. She was rubbing Mr Collins's name out from Josh's column. Sophie sensed her hesitating under Oliver's name. St David's junior partner had been quite clear about his own instructions regarding this patient.

What the hell? Sophie decided. 'I'll see Mr Collins,' she told Toni.

Toni's jaw dropped. 'Are you kidding?'

'No.' If she didn't see Mr Collins, she would have to go and talk to Oliver. Right now, Mr Collins seemed a far more attractive option. He looked quite benign, really, sitting in the far corner of the waiting room. Almost completely bald, he had just a ring of white fluff beneath a very red scalp. Mr Collins was fat, and when he stood up to follow Sophie she discovered that his shiny head came only to her shoulder. Mr Collins looked exactly like a leprechaun. The most alarming thing about the elderly gentleman was the very large paper bag he was carrying.

'It won't be difficult for you, lassie.' The volume of Mr Collins's voice was out of all proportion to his height. He parked the bag beside his chair in Sophie's consulting room. 'It's a UTI,' he bellowed. He peered short-sightedly at Sophie. 'Are you a nurse?'

'No, I'm a doctor. I'm a GP registrar.'

'Bit young, aren't you?' Mr Collins shouted. 'Never mind. I know what I'm on about. A UTI is a urinary tract infection.'

'Yes, I know.' Sophie leaned over her desk. 'Are you wearing a hearing aid, Mr Collins?'

'What? Speak up, girl. I'm a bit deaf.'

'Have you turned on your hearing aid?' Sophie asked loudly.

Mr Collins fiddled with his ear and then peered at Sophie. 'Say that again, lassie. I'm turned on now.'

Sophie closed her eyes briefly at the thought, then she spoke slowly and clearly. 'What makes you think you might have a urinary tract infection, Mr Collins?'

'I don't *think*. I know.' Mr Collins shook his head despairingly. 'You just write me a prescription, young lady. A broad-spectrum antibiotic, I think. Let's try some Bactrim. I had a bit of a skin reaction to the Amoxil I had last time.'

'I can't prescribe antibiotics unless you need them, Mr Collins,' Sophie stated firmly. 'What are your symptoms?'

'What?'

'Are you running a temperature? Do you have pain on passing urine? Do you—?'

'Pain? Of course I've got pain.' Mr Collins glared at Sophie. 'It's the cysts.'

'Pardon?' Sophie blinked in surprise.

'Are you deaf as well, lassie? *Cysts*!' Mr Collins boomed. 'In my piddle. See?' With a rapid yank, he reached into the paper bag, lifted a two-litre plastic milk container filled with yellowish fluid and plonked it onto Sophie's desk. She shrank backwards.

'I brought a sample.' Mr Collins's chin jutted proudly. 'I always bring a sample.'

'Hmmm.' Sophie eyed the container. She bit her lip hard and tried to keep her face straight. 'How long did it take to collect this sample, Mr Collins?'

'Not long,' he responded airily. 'Couple of days.' He picked up the bottle by the handle and shook it briskly. Sophie cringed, hoping fervently that the lid was screwed on tightly. 'Look at that!' Mr Collins crowed in delight. 'Cysts. Millions of the little buggers.'

Sophie caught a glimpse of the disturbed sediment

before she shut her eyes again. 'Did you rinse the container before you started collecting your sample, Mr Collins?'

'I gave it a bit of a swirl.' Sophie could sense that her patient was peering at her again. 'Are you tired, girl? Not up to the job, eh? Perhaps I'd better see one of the proper doctors.'

Sophie opened her eyes smartly. 'I'm fine,' she said firmly. 'Tell me, Mr Collins, did your pain on passing urine start before or after you began using this container?'

'After.' Mr Collins leered at Sophie. 'It was a bit of a tight fit, you know.'

'Leave it with me,' Sophie told him carefully. 'We'll test it and I'll get back to you if you need to take some antibiotics.'

She had to get herself a glass of water. Either that or bury her face in a cushion and shriek with laughter. Gingerly, Sophie transferred the impressive sample of Mr Collins's urine to the staffroom. She hadn't expected to find anyone in there but the courier, Ross, was downing a drink of water.

'I needed that,' he told Sophie. 'High-pressure job, this.' He looked at the milk container Sophie was holding and his expression changed. He looked at his empty glass and hurriedly put it into the sink.

'Hi, Ross. How's the back?' Sophie opened the sample fridge but there was no room for the large bottle. She closed it again.

'Great, thanks, Doc.' Ross watched Sophie deliberate over where to put her burden. 'Can I tell you something?'

'Sure.' Sophie eyed the rubbish bin longingly.

'I'm just bursting to tell someone.' Ross had a grin

that stretched from ear to ear. 'I'm going to be a father.'

'Really? Congratulations.' Sophie wondered if it might be something in the air.

'It's fantastic, isn't it? Not that we're married yet, but that doesn't matter these days, does it?'

'Not at all, Ross.' Definitely something in the air, Sophie decided. She discounted the possibility of leaving the bottle on the bench.

'We'll be inviting you to the wedding, of course, Doc.'

Sophie forgot the bottle. 'Really? That's sweet of you, Ross, but—'

'We'll be inviting all the St David's staff. After all, it would never have happened if we hadn't met here.'

Sophie eyed the air-conditioning unit. Surely not. 'I had no idea,' she said distractedly.

'It's nearly a year ago now,' Ross told her happily. 'I was running in with a parcel for Doc Spencer and I flattened her. She took quite a tumble down the ramp.'

'Oh, dear.'

'It was her first day on the job, too. She was really upset.'

'I'll bet.' Sophie wanted to escape. Ross was exuding so much happiness she felt stifled. 'What does she do?'

'She's a drug rep.' Ross frowned at Sophie's blank expression. 'You must know her. Christine. Christine Prescott.' He grinned. 'Soon to be Christine Selkirk.'

'And you've been going out with her for a *year*?'

'Hell, we've been living together for a year. Things took off pretty fast. We couldn't get enough of each other. Still can't. The only time we're apart is when

she has to travel and that's going to stop as soon as
we're married.' Ross tossed another grin at Sophie.
'Better go. Time is money and I'm going to be a dad
soon.'

Sophie only remembered the weighty item still
dangling from her hand after Ross had gone. She
placed it carefully in the centre of the dining table.
She stood very still, trying to analyse how she felt. It
was rather hard to put a name to the violent emotions
roiling through her at that moment, but fury was probably paramount. She picked up the staffroom phone,
dialling 1 to put her through to the reception area.

'Toni? Has Oliver got a patient with him?'

'No. Mr Laney just came out. I was about to send
Mrs Chamberlain in but Janet needs to take a BP and
so on. Might take a few minutes. She loves to talk.'

'Good. Let her take as long as she likes,' Sophie
suggested with deceptive calm. 'Is Mrs Wentworth
still asleep?'

'She's snoring,' Toni reported. 'Shall I wake her
up?'

'Not yet.' Sophie still sounded calm. 'I need to
have a word with Oliver.'

She put the receiver down carefully, then turned
mechanically. Sophie Bennett had never felt so furious in her whole life. She was ready to explode, and
if she didn't move very, very carefully, she might do
just that.

Her measured steps took her to Oliver's door. She
turned the handle slowly and stepped into his office.
The temptation to slam the door shut behind her was
stifled by the same icy calm she now focused on
Oliver Spencer.

'You lied to me,' she enunciated very clearly.
'You—of all people! You *lied* to me!'

CHAPTER TEN

OLIVER SPENCER didn't look in the least bit ashamed of himself.

He seemed rather taken aback by the furious verbal assault Sophie had launched. Taken aback, but not in the least bit guilty or dismayed at having been caught out. He leaned back in his chair in a surprisingly relaxed fashion.

'When, precisely, did I lie to you, Sophie?'

'When you told me you were having an affair with Christine Prescott.'

Oliver shook his head. 'I did not tell you at any time that I was having an affair with Christine Prescott. You *assumed* I was.'

'You encouraged me to make that assumption.'

Oliver shrugged. 'I didn't lie directly.'

'Oh, so that makes it all right, does it?' Sophie's tone was heavily sarcastic.

'You tell me, Sophie.'

Sophie took a step towards Oliver. She leaned over his desk. 'As far as I'm concerned, it doesn't make a blind bit of difference, Oliver Spencer. You deceived me. And, what's more, I think you enjoyed doing it.'

'I wouldn't say that.' Oliver shook his head in rapid denial. 'Maybe at first, when I could see that it bothered you, but you really shook me up yesterday. I didn't realise how deception could take over. How difficult it might be to put things right.' He rubbed his chin. 'Let me tell you, Sophie. I didn't get much sleep last night.'

Sophie's lip curled fractionally. 'My heart bleeds,' she muttered. She narrowed her eyes. 'I wondered whether you were lying, right from the start. Well, from when Christine said her weekends hadn't been up to scratch. But then I thought, No way! If there's one person in the world who understands the damage lying can do, it's Oliver Spencer.'

'Quite right.' Instead of being ashamed or guilty or even taken aback now, Oliver looked curiously happy. His voice remained serious, however. 'Maybe I thought it was time somebody else learned as well.'

'Who?'

'You.' Oliver regarded Sophie steadily. 'Why did you lie to *me*, Sophie? About your engagement.'

'I didn't lie. Not exactly.'

'No. You let me assume. You did lie about that message on the card, though, didn't you. You did lie about your wedding date?'

'You already know that,' Sophie muttered.

'So you were doing your own bit of deception, weren't you? Maybe *you* enjoyed it. Maybe you weren't even engaged to Graham.'

'*Greg*,' Sophie seethed. 'And I *was* engaged.'

'Oh? Up until when?'

'Up until I went to Auckland for the weekend. That's when I broke it off.' Sophie tried to keep up her furious stare but her eyes shifted away from Oliver's involuntarily. She had come in to accuse Oliver of dishonesty. Now she seemed to be in the witness box. How had he managed that so neatly?

'Ah!' Oliver's mouth pursed thoughtfully. 'So you

broke it off before those flowers arrived. Why were you still wearing your ring, then?'

Sophie failed miserably in her attempt to look nonchalant. 'I took it off the next day,' she pointed out defensively.

'And you lied about that, too,' Oliver announced cheerfully. 'Why did you do that, Sophie? Were you scared to admit how you really felt?'

Sophie refused to meet Oliver's gaze. She heard him clear his throat.

'I was only trying to play by your rules, Sophie,' Oliver told her mildly. 'I didn't muscle in when I thought you were engaged. I tried to give you some space. I even gave due consideration to your suggestion that I find someone who might appreciate my kind of charm.'

'So I'm responsible for your deception?' Sophie let her breath out in an incredulous huff. 'You thought I was playing the same game you were?' Her voice rose angrily. 'Relationships between people aren't games, Oliver. They're serious.'

'I was being serious,' Oliver said calmly. 'I wanted you to realise I was capable of more than the shallow relationship you seem to think men like me want. I wanted you to know that I'm interested in commitment now. Even marriage. Children.' Oliver nodded with satisfaction. 'Especially children. And a house with a nice big garden.'

Sophie ignored the dreamy look on Oliver's face. She was outraged. 'So you do it by playing games?' she snapped. 'By manipulating people?'

Oliver sighed. 'Look, I know I've gone about this the wrong way. I realised that yesterday and that's why I stayed up half the night, trying to ring you. It

seemed like a good plan but it got a bit out of hand.'
Oliver ran his fingers through his hair. 'I didn't know
what else to do at the time, Sophie. I'd tried letting
you know how I felt, without scaring you off, but you
thought it was all a joke. I haven't had much experience with women like you. Serious women.' Oliver
smiled placatingly. 'Would it help if I said I was
sorry? That I was blinded by love?'

'Huh!' Sophie said scornfully. 'I don't think you've
got the faintest idea what love is all about.'

'Don't I?'

'No. People who love each other don't play
games.'

'Don't they?' Oliver looked disappointed. 'What,
never? Why not? Can't love be fun sometimes?'

'They don't play games with each other's feelings.'
Sophie geared her tone to that of a parent reproving
a rather difficult child. The man was being insuffer-
ably and deliberately obtuse. He almost looked as
though he was enjoying himself. 'They don't set out
to make people jealous,' she finished triumphantly.

'So you *were* jealous?'

Sophie glared at Oliver stonily.

'You made *me* jealous,' Oliver told her sombrely.
'But I forgive you,' he added magnanimously. He ran
his fingers through his hair with an agitated movement and stood up suddenly. 'What *can* I do to con-
vince you?'

'Try telling the truth,' Sophie suggested coolly.

Oliver cast her a hopeful glance. 'I will if you will.'

Sophie nodded after a second's pause. 'Sounds
fair.'

'OK.' Oliver stood very still. He was several feet
away from Sophie but his gaze made direct contact.

The dark grey eyes were soft. Indisputably sincere. 'I love you, Sophie Bennett. I am not remotely interested in any other woman. I never could be. I want to share my life with you. I want to marry you.' Oliver paused then drew in a long and rather shaky breath. He smiled crookedly. 'Your turn,' he prompted gruffly.

But Sophie couldn't speak. She was blinking hard to try and clear her vision. She was swallowing hard to try and clear the lump in her throat. She had to say something. Oliver was waiting patiently. She could see the depth of emotion in his face, even though it was blurred by her tears. He looked achingly vulnerable. He had spoken the truth and was afraid of the potential rejection. A rejection Sophie could never issue.

'I want to marry you, too,' she whispered finally. And then she burst into tears.

Sophie was aware that Oliver was moving closer. He was reaching out towards her. He was...

He was taking her in his arms. Kissing her damp lashes, her cheeks, her forehead, even her chin, before his lips gently touched hers.

'I love you,' he said again.

'I love you, too,' Sophie said shyly. It was the first time she had spoken those words aloud to this man. The first time she had known just how much those words could mean.

Oliver's lips touched hers again, softly. Then the kiss deepened. If any confirmation was needed of how they really felt about each other, this kiss said it all. Neither of them heard the tap on the door. They only just heard the end of Toni's query.

'Ready for Mrs Chamberlain now? *Oh!*'

Oliver and Sophie surfaced. Oliver's arms tightened around Sophie and she could feel the wave of heat flooding her face as she caught Toni's stunned expression.

'Not just yet, Toni,' Oliver said evenly. 'I'm dealing with a minor emergency here.'

Toni's mouth opened and closed soundlessly. She tried again. 'I'll...I'll make Mrs Chamberlain a cup of tea, shall I?'

'Excellent idea,' Oliver said approvingly. He watched the door close again. 'Now, where were we? I know.' He pulled Sophie gently after him and sat down on his chair, drawing her onto his lap. His smile was as gentle as his touch. 'When you went away to Auckland for the weekend I tortured myself, imagining another man sharing the rest of your life. It was then I realised I had to find some way of convincing you that you felt the same way.'

'So you presented me with the scenario of you and Christine Prescott riding off into the sunset—complete with a picket fence in the distance.'

Oliver grinned. 'Not a great plan, was it?'

Sophie tried to look stern. 'The worst,' she informed him, 'but at least your motive was honourable.'

They were grinning at each other as another tap on the door heralded Josh's entry. He looked as stunned as Toni at the sight of Sophie sitting on Oliver's lap. Then he smiled broadly. 'Looks like I'm interrupting something.'

'You are,' Oliver confirmed. 'Go away.'

'Right. Consider me gone.' Josh was still grinning. 'But can one of you tell me what that is in the bottle on our dining table?'

Sophie groaned. 'Sorry. I shouldn't have put it there. I think it can be thrown out. It's a...' Sophie suppressed a wild giggle. 'It's a urine sample.'

There was short silence. Then Oliver and Josh spoke together. 'Mr Collins?'

'Mr Collins.' Sophie nodded.

Oliver and Josh both laughed, then Josh shook his head. 'You've had your initiation now, Sophie. You've really made it into the partnership.'

'No, she hasn't,' Oliver told him. 'But we're getting there. Or we will if you'll just leave us alone.'

'I'm gone,' Josh said quickly. He was still grinning as his face disappeared behind the closing door.

Oliver's grip tightened around Sophie but she pulled back a little.

'Why did you tell me to sort things out with Greg? I thought you were telling me you weren't interested after all.'

Oliver sighed heavily. 'I knew if you felt anything like I did then there was no way you were going to marry someone else. I needed you to know that as well.'

Sophie tilted her head. 'You certainly tried hard, even if your plan was a bit warped. I suppose it even worked,' she conceded. 'In its own way.'

'I didn't think it was going to work at all,' Oliver confessed. 'I could have strangled Christine for saying her weekends hadn't been up to scratch.'

'I could have strangled her, too,' Sophie declared. 'Especially after you produced those wedding invitations.'

'Inspired, weren't they?' The twinkle was back in Oliver's grey eyes. 'I told the others they were in for a surprise. Do you want to go public with an announcement yet?'

Sophie grinned. 'I think we already have. Janet's the only person who hasn't been in to visit us.'

Oliver leaned forward to place a lingering kiss on Sophie's lips. She was startled when he lifted his head abruptly.

'I want a really short engagement,' he told her sternly. 'None of this five-year nonsense.'

'Let's skip being engaged, then,' Sophie suggested. 'Let's just get married.'

'Right.' Oliver's eyes gleamed purposefully. 'Let's get the invitations out and pick one. If you really love those cupids I'm prepared to sacrifice the doves.'

Sophie laughed. 'Let's get on with seeing our patients. I'm sure Mrs Chamberlain has finished two cups of tea by now and Mrs Wentworth has slept quite long enough.'

Oliver reluctantly let go of Sophie. 'The deal still stands, though, doesn't it?'

'What deal?' Sophie straightened her skirt as she stood up. 'That I'll tell the truth if you do?'

'I will never lie to you, Sophie. And I won't play any more games. Not about important things.'

Sophie smiled. 'I wouldn't want you to stop having fun, Oliver. Just make sure I'm on the same team next time.'

'It's a deal.' Oliver nodded. 'Now, what about our other deal? The one we made ages ago?'

'What was that?'

'You invite me to your wedding and I'll invite you to mine.'

Sophie looked nonplussed then her lips curved slowly. 'Same day?'

'Same day,' Oliver nodded.

'Same time?'

'Of course.'

'Same place?'

'Absolutely.' Oliver was grinning. 'And the same people. You and me, Sophie Bennett. Our wedding.' His face stilled. 'Is it a deal?'

Sophie indulged in several seconds of bliss, registering the love and hope she saw in Oliver's eyes. She knew her own face must be reflecting the same depth of feeling. Finally, she nodded solemnly.

'It's a deal.'

*Look next month for the touching story of
Toni Marsh and Josh Cooper in*
THE PERFECT RESULT.

MILLS & BOON®

Makes any time special™

Mills & Boon publish 29 new titles every month. Select from...

Modern Romance™   **Tender Romance™**

Sensual Romance™

Medical Romance™   Historical Romance™

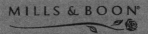

MILLS & BOON®

Medical Romance™

JUST A FAMILY DOCTOR *by Caroline Anderson*

Audley Memorial

Allie Baker's new job as Staff Nurse at Audley Memorial Hospital brought her back into contact with Senior Houseman Mark Jarvis. Love blossomed until she found out he was going to become a GP—a profession she had sworn never to marry into…

ONE AND ONLY *by Josie Metcalfe*

First of a Trilogy

The victim of a childhood custody battle, Cassie Mills had vowed never to be second best. But Dr Luke Thornton needed her help to fight for custody of his baby daughter. Could she put her past behind her and be Luke's future?

A PERFECT RESULT *by Alison Roberts*

Second of a Trilogy

Although practice manager Toni Marsh loved her job at St David's Medical Centre and its senior partner, Josh Cooper, she realised it was time to leave. Unrequited love was no fun.

On sale 6th October 2000

0009/03a

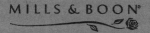

Medical Romance™

LIFTING SUSPICION *by Gill Sanderson*

Third of a Trilogy

All Megan Taylor had ever wanted was to be a good doctor and now her reputation was at stake. Would consultant Charles Grant-Liffley believe her side of the story…

PARTNERS FOR LIFE *by Lucy Clark*

First of a Duo

Angus O'Donnell has agreed to locum for Janet McNeil, a childhood friend. Having not seen each other for eight years, Janet is amazed to discover how attractive she finds this new Angus…

DIVIDED LOYALTIES *by Joanna Neil*

Dr Caitlin Burnett is determined to secure a new job in Ecuador so she can be near her brother who is in a coma following an accident. Her new boss, Dr Nick Garcia, wants a committed employee so Caitlin decides to hide the truth…for now.

On sale 6th October 2000

Available at most branches of WH Smith, Tesco, Martins, Borders, Easons, Volume One/James Thin and most good paperback bookshops

0009/03b

For better, for worse... for ever

Brides and Grooms

FREE
4 BOOKS
AND A SURPRISE GIFT!

We would like to take this opportunity to thank you for reading this Mills & Boon® book by offering you the chance to take FOUR more specially selected titles from the Medical Romance™ series absolutely FREE! We're also making this offer to introduce you to the benefits of the Reader Service™—

- ★ FREE home delivery
- ★ FREE monthly Newsletter
- ★ FREE gifts and competitions
- ★ Exclusive Reader Service discounts
- ★ Books available before they're in the shops

Accepting these FREE books and gift places you under no obligation to buy; you may cancel at any time, even after receiving your free shipment. Simply complete your details below and return the entire page to the address below. *You don't even need a stamp!*

YES! Please send me 4 free Medical Romance books and a surprise gift. I understand that unless you hear from me, I will receive 6 superb new titles every month for just £2.40 each, postage and packing free. I am under no obligation to purchase any books and may cancel my subscription at any time. The free books and gift will be mine to keep in any case.

M0ZEC

Ms/Mrs/Miss/Mr ....Initials ....

BLOCK CAPITALS PLEASE

Surname ....

Address ....

....

....Postcode ....

Send this whole page to:
UK: FREEPOST CN81, Croydon, CR9 3WZ
EIRE: PO Box 4546, Kilcock, County Kildare (stamp required)